CHASED

CLARISSA WILD

Copyright © 2018 Clarissa Wild
All rights reserved.
ISBN: 978-1984307453
ISBN-10: 1984307452

This is a work of fiction. Names, characters, places and incidents are either the product of the author's imagination or are used fictitiously. Any resemblance to actual events, places, organizations, or person, whether living or dead, is entirely coincidental.

All rights reserved. No part of this book may be reproduced, transmitted in any form or by any means, electronic or mechanical, including photocopying, recording, or by any information storage retrieval system. Doing so would break licensing and copyright laws.

ONE

CHASE

From my comfy seat, I glare at the squabbling men across the room, waiting until the light above the door switches on. The anticipation is starting to unnerve me.

Rummaging through my pocket, I take out a notebook and a pen, and start outlining their faces, depicting what they look like, observing every minute detail. I write down everything important—from greasy hair, to curly mustaches, to eye color, to fat bellies, and pockets stuffed with checks.

Some of them aren't even wearing masks.

Stupid fucks.

When I'm done, I tuck away the notebook, grab my whiskey on the rocks, and take a sip.

Am I really going to do this?

Yes, yes, I am.

The grip of my hand almost breaks the glass, so I put it down before I hurt myself. I get up and march straight to the bathroom, where I turn on the faucet and let the water cascade over my hands.

I stare down at the water and at my fingers.

Soon, they'll probably be drenched in blood.

I close my eyes and take a deep breath.

This is it, Chase.

This is the moment you've waited your entire life for.

You're going to do this whether you like it or not. End of story.

I look up at the man staring back at me in the mirror. Or rather ... the shiny, plastic, metallic mask covering my face.

It's a stark reminder of who I really am.

I'm not the man hiding behind the mask.

The mask *is* me.

The man behind it just a mere figment of my imagination.

He's the man who has it all ... and it still isn't enough.

This mask brings out the animal in me, the one hiding in plain sight.

And no one will ever know it was me.

I smile to myself, thinking about what's to come. Whatever choice I make, it's sure to be a spectacle. One I won't forget anytime soon.

As I open the door to step back into the room again, the

light above the door turns on, and the men stop talking. They glance briefly at me as I march toward them and wait for the door to open. When it does, they direct their attention to the room beyond.

We all sit on small black chairs lining the red walls. In the back are three metal cages, each containing a person. Two women, one man.

They're trembling, huddled in a corner, clutching their bodies.

All wearing the same red-colored underwear that barely covers any skin, save for the sensitive parts.

They whimper and cower away from the lights aimed at them. But I can't help stare at just one of them ... a girl to my right with the most beautiful, dark curly hair I've seen in a long while.

The cages are behind thick, impenetrable glass, with only one door leading inside.

I doubt they can see us ... but all the men can definitely see them.

"Welcome, gentlemen. I hope you all enjoyed the whiskey while waiting," a voice in the corner says as he approaches.

Graham.

My fists ball as he talks.

"Take a good look. All three of them are available. If you win, the prize will be delivered via the back door after the bidding ends with an added fifteen to twenty minutes to account for transportation. Same door you came in through.

Now, I'll begin with number one on the left shortly. Any questions?"

He gazes around the room, but no one responds.

It's not as if they haven't done this before.

Many, many times.

Grinding my teeth, I sit back in the chair and continue to stare at the girl on the right. It's going to be her.

I've already decided.

"Okay." Graham clears his throat. "The first one's a little stubborn, but he responds well to punishment. He's deaf on one side, but the other ear works perfectly. No other defects. He's virile and young, perfect for working with his hands, such as personal grooming, housekeeping, or general entertainment. Whatever you want."

The smirk on his face is murderous.

It makes *me* feel murderous.

I can't help it. I'm a savage in a suit who enjoys dishing out pain.

But now is not the right time.

Graham pushes a button, and the male on the left is buzzed so hard he rolls around across the floor of his cage, his face contorted and gasping for air. I look away.

"Up!" Graham yells through an intercom.

The kid struggles to stand but does it anyway. Then he bangs his head against the bars until Graham releases the button, after which he just stands there, motionless … staring right at the glass separating us.

"Bidding starts at twenty thousand."

The men raise their fingers as Graham announces increasing numbers. I ignore their voices and focus solely on the girl on the right. For some reason, she's gotten up from her corner and walked all the way up to the front. Graham didn't even have to buzz her to get her to move.

She clutches tightly to the bars surrounding her. She's not looking at us, yet I still feel watched. As if she can hear us. Or like she's trying to.

"Fifty thousand, going once, going twice. Sold!" The bidder on the far right hands a check to Graham who inspects it before shaking his hand. "Thank you."

He walks back to the center and says, "Okay ... next one is a female. She's ripe, of age, and perfect for any party or gathering. She's very sociable and listens to commands well. Also has an implant for ultimate pleasure."

Graham presses another button on the wall, making her squirm in her cage. She jumps to her feet without him having to say a word. The buzzing stops ... but he reaches into his pocket and takes out a device, clicking it on.

She clenches her legs, and her cheeks flush. A slight mewl leaves her mouth.

The men chuckle, throwing glances at each other, gloating like crazy.

I swallow and loosen my collar, then stare at my hands. They're covered in marks from my nails digging into my skin.

"Bidding begins at thirty thousand."

The men bid again, but I can only focus on one thing.

The girl on the right ... Her eyes and how they rise to meet mine, only for just a second.

They're so ... clear. And beautiful.

In her cage, she sinks to the floor and lowers her head, hiding her face among her curly hair.

I have to focus on her and only her.

If not, I'd probably outbid every man in this room until I won all three.

But that would only make things harder for me.

I have to be patient. Have to be wary. Have to fit in.

So I wait and wait until the bidding finishes at seventy thousand, after which another check is exchanged.

Finally, it's time.

"Lastly, we have a short but spicy female. This one particularly gave me a lot of trouble."

The men in the room snigger.

But I don't find it funny. Not one bit.

"She's spunky, but with a bit of training, she'll make a wonderful pet. However, there is a small defect ... she is blind."

Blind? No wonder her eyes are so ... pretty.

A grin spreads across my lips.

This couldn't be any more perfect.

Graham presses another button. She's crippled with fear and pain, crawling in her cage, but she doesn't give up. Doesn't stop clutching the bars, doesn't get up.

"Up!" Graham yells.

I clench my fists, watching her struggle. She refuses to

give up the fight even though she's already lost by a long shot. She's in a cage, yet her spirit never fails her.

I admire her.

But I also wish she'd just surrender.

"Please ..." I mutter to myself, biting my lip.

Only after a grueling minute has passed does she finally relent.

She's light on her feet, but oh so unsteady.

"Bidding starts at fifteen thousand."

I run my fingers along my jaw, staring at the girl, while the men start to bid.

For a moment, I stop breathing and focus entirely on her feeble body, which seems to be able to withstand so much pain. It's incredible.

When the men stop muttering their bids, I raise my hand.

"One million."

Everyone looks at me with gaping mouths. As if I've lost my mind.

But they don't know what she's worth. They can't see it ... but I do.

To me, she is *everything*.

Her existence will be my downfall or my only salvation.

I have to know which one it's going to be.

I *have* to have her.

"Any other bids?" Graham asks, hoping someone will bid more.

Of course, not. They don't want her. They don't see the

use in a blind, defiant girl.

But I do.

"Okay … going once. Going twice. Sold!" Graham says, and he approaches me.

I narrow my eyes at him and cock my head while I take my sweet time rummaging through my pocket to conjure up a checkbook. With quick scribbles, I write everything he needs. I don't look twice before tearing it off and handing it to him.

"Thank you," he says, greedily snatching it away from me. Then he directs his attention toward the rest. "Well, that was all. I'll have more for you next time."

Everyone gets up and leaves, but not me.

With careful steps, I approach the glass and place my hand on top of it, wishing I could already touch her. I wonder what I'll feel. What I'll want. What she smells like. How she'll taste.

I close my eyes and imagine all those things.

Riveting.

"I'll bring her to you in a moment," Graham says. "You bid quite a lot."

I smile and look his way. "I know what I want. And I always get what I want."

He smiles back awkwardly and then clears his throat. "All right. Well, if you will please wait in the other room like the others, I'll get to work."

I nod and take my hand off the glass, saying a mental goodbye before turning around and walking back outside.

***

Syrena

In a wheelchair, I'm wheeled out of the cage. I don't know what's happening because my mind is barely there. All I know is that I've been drugged ... heavily.

I feel numb. When I wiggle my toes, nothing happens, and my fingers don't respond either. All I can do is wait for my fate.

Will I even get to say goodbye to Ella and Cage?

Before Graham put me in the cage beside these two, I was in a different place. Somewhere upstairs in a glass cage, right next to two other people. But at least I had an actual bed and privacy there.

Not here. Here ... I was only a doll put up for sale.

Ella and Cage were my original cellmates, but now they already feel like distant memories.

I'm forced to close and open new chapters in my life in rapid succession, and I can't keep up.

So much has happened these past few months that I feel as if I'm beginning to lose my mind.

Captured by a monster, then stuffed in a glass prison with two other people, and now, I'm being taken from the compound where I've been living for months.

Where will I go?

And more importantly ... will I ever get back home again?

A tear manages to leave my eyes and roll down my cheek as Graham sets me down and leaves.

Moments later, I can hear the groaning of two other people right beside me. The girl and the boy who were beside me in the cage just now.

I don't even know who they are. This is probably the last time we'll meet.

No one talks. A door creaks. Then Graham pushes us forward, one by one. A man clears his throat. Someone else shuffles around. I wonder how many there are.

Moments like these are when I really hate being blind.

The longer I sit in this chair, the more I begin to feel my arms and legs again, and my lips can definitely move. I don't talk, though. I don't want to give Graham incentive to sedate me again.

"You can take the wheelchair with you. It's on the house," Graham says.

I wonder who he's talking to.

Is this person the next one to keep me as a prisoner?

Probably.

Still, it makes me shiver in place.

Suddenly, a hand on my hand makes me freeze.

"Syrena."

I look up even though I can't see. His voice centers me,

forces me to find him. It's commanding but scary. Daring and completely in control.

"Graham told me that's your name. Is it correct?"

I nod slowly.

Something pushes my wheelchair along. I'm assuming it's him.

"Great. Then let's go."

I don't know what happened to the others, but I assume the other men are taking them with them.

The man pushes me outside, through a corridor, turns right, then another turn, and then we stop. A door squeaks, and a warm glow meets my face. Not soon after, he pushes me outside, and the sun's rays heat my skin. I bask in it. I open my mouth and let the fresh air enter my lungs. Tears run down my cheeks.

"No need to cry. I'll take … good care of you," he says, his voice dark and foreboding.

I don't think I can trust anything he says.

However, I'm happy to finally be outside the compound again.

So much time has passed since I last smelled the dry air. God, how I've missed it.

He pushes me across rocky terrain until we come to a stop, and I hear the beeps of a car.

A door slides open. "Hey."

It's a new voice.

"Get her in," the man who pushed me says.

Suddenly, I'm lifted out of my seat and lifted into the

car, landing on a soft cushion. Someone straps me in with a seat belt and closes the door. Another door on my other side opens, and someone sits down beside me.

The other person throws the wheelchair in the trunk and then sits down behind the wheel.

"No need to worry …" It's him, right beside me, whispering in my ear.

I suck in a breath.

I want to scream, but I can't. I physically can't. The only things leaving my throat are a tiny squeal and some rasps. "The drugs will wear off soon."

I hope so because I really, really want to get out of here.

Now that I've had a taste of freedom … it feels too good to be true.

I'm so close. I only have to move my hands to the door and open it.

But the familiar click of the locks sinks my heart to my shoes.

"Let's go," the man besides me barks at the one behind the wheel, and the car begins to drive across the rocky terrain.

"Who … who are you?" I ask after a while, as the drugs begin to fade around my lips and throat.

The man beside me hums and puts his hand on mine as it rests in my lap. "Call me Chase… your new owner."

TWO

CHASE

The first thing I do when we get far enough away is take off the mask. Finally, I can breathe.

It's deadly quiet as we drive.

It's not a coincidence.

Whatever Graham gave her to keep her meek still has the girl paralyzed. But that won't last much longer.

It's mostly Brandon whose silent treatment doesn't even make me flinch.

He keeps glancing my way, raising his brow, as if it will make me speak.

I know what he's thinking, what he wants from me, but I'm not gonna give it to him.

I'm dead set on doing this.

The second I set foot inside that compound, I'd already sold my soul to the devil.

Nothing will change that.

Nothing.

Not even his venomous glares.

"There's still time," Brandon says, grinding his teeth.

A smirk spreads across my lips as I rub them. Oh, lord … he really can't stop himself, can he? Self-righteous prick.

"I know," I say, biting the insides of my cheeks.

"We can keep driving," he adds.

"No."

I gaze outside at the barren wasteland, counting down the seconds until we arrive at our destination. It isn't far from here. Not too long now and I'll finally know the truth.

The girl next to me groans. It's time to switch.

"Stop."

Brandon does what I ask, and I quickly exit the car and get into the passenger's seat. "Lock the doors."

He tsks me but does it without saying anything else. The look he's giving me is enough. I know what he's thinking, but I don't care.

He starts the car again, but before he drives off, he mumbles, "Chase …."

"No. Drive."

I keep deflecting his attempts to sway me. There's no use. I made up my mind a long time ago.

This must be done. Whether he likes it or not.

"I know I promised to help, but don't you think this has gone far enough?"

"No. I need to do this."

"But she's just a kid," he says.

"She's not, and you know that. Don't try to use lies against me. It won't work." I say, gazing at myself in the side mirror.

I cock my head and run my finger along the small indent in my chin. My skin feels tense. *I am* tense. I just don't want to admit it, and no one needs to know because it'll only make this more difficult than it needs to be.

"Are you sure?" he asks, as if I can still change my mind.

It's way too late for that.

"Yes," I reply, setting his mind at ease. Not mine.

"Fine. But don't say I didn't warn you." He clears his throat, like he's so high and mighty.

"You know why this has to be done," I say, looking his way.

"Really? Does it have to?"

"Yes. You would too if you were me."

"No, I wouldn't."

I raise a brow. "Did you forget we're playing the same game?"

"I'm just looking out for both our interests. I'm not gonna pick you up off the ground when you ruin yourself. No way."

"I didn't ask you to."

"But you're asking me to just sit here and watch."

"Then close your eyes." I shrug. "Simple."

He narrows his eyes. "I'm driving."

"You know what I mean." I wave it away.

A groan emanates from the back, and I turn my head only to smile. The drugs are wearing off.

"It's time."

"We're not there yet."

I quickly roll up the privacy partition between the front seats and the back. "Drive faster."

As we drive across the rocky, uneven terrain, the girl starts to move around, calling out in desperation, but I try not to pay any attention. Doing so will only make this harder. I want to go at this with a clear mind. I don't want emotions to weigh me down, so I refuse to have any.

It doesn't take the girl long to start banging on the window.

"Who are you people? Where are you taking me?"

She'll know the answer soon.

We're already approaching the area. I can see the bushes and deep canyon from here, and it won't be long until we are outside, sniffing the fresh air.

And animals.

"Let me out!" the girl squeaks, kicking the car door.

My skin crawls, so I cover up my arms by pulling down my sleeves.

Brandon drives down the canyon across a gravelly path until we're in the middle of nowhere, and he stops the car.

I straighten my collar and clear my throat.

Judgment time.

The girl is still banging on the window between us, so I guess she's recovered. Good.

I get out.

"Chase." I pause and look at Brandon. "Don't do this."

I slam the door shut.

I don't need his opinion right now. It's an added weight I can't carry right now. I need to do this on my own terms.

Two steps and I come face to face with the blind girl. Syrena. But I'm not nearly as excited as I imagined I'd be. My smile immediately disappears at the sight of her.

So help me God ... I will do this, no matter if it is the end of me.

I'll accept whatever fate brings.

***

Syrena

I hold my breath as the door slams shut and another one opens. My body ceases moving the moment the door disappears from under my feet as I was kicking it. *He* opened it.

Is he letting me out?

Should I take my chance and run?

No time to waste, but what do I do? Fight him?

"Before you get anything in your head ... don't."

Was that a threat? Is he carrying a weapon? I swallow away the lump in my throat.

I have to be careful around him. I don't know this man.

I didn't know Graham either, but at least I understood his patterns, his behavior ... after a while.

But this? This is something entirely different.

I've been taken out of my cage, out of the compound, driven somewhere in a car of which I don't recognize the smell. None of this is familiar to me, which makes it all the more frightening.

Moments such as these are when I miss the ability to see the most.

When it's fight or flight.

"What do you want from me?" I ask, my voice quaking with fear I don't want him to hear.

He snorts and says, "Give me your hand."

I contemplate whether to trust him. What's the worst that can happen? If he wanted to kill me, he could use any weapon he has. Doesn't need his hands to do it. So it must be safe ... right?

I hesitate but then hold out my hand anyway, and he pulls me out of the car.

"Strong enough to stand?" he asks.

I nod.

"To run?"

I suck in a breath.

Run? Why?

"Answer me." His voice is commanding. Not at all sweet. There's nothing poking at my back, no gun, but the sound of his growl is enough to make me do whatever he wants.

"Yes," I say, feeling the power return to my legs.

"Good ..." he murmurs. "Show me."

"What? Now?"

"Yes," he groans. I'm suddenly aware of how close he is to my ears. "Run."

A shiver runs up and down my spine. "Where?"

"Away ... *from me.*"

I shake my head as my hands touch the car, and I immediately jump back and turn around.

I don't understand ... why does he want me to run away from him?

But more importantly ... what is he going to do me?

I don't wait to find out.

I immediately start running.

It wasn't his words that pulled the trigger. Or the car. Or the need in my bones to get away.

It was the sheer delight in his voice when he told me I needed to run from *him*.

I bounce across the ground, kicking away the rocks as best as I can, even though I can't see them coming. As a blind girl, I've learned how to run while holding my feet as firmly to the ground as I possibly can so I don't slip.

Still, I can't avoid everything, and a sudden big rock

trips me, and I fall.

My knees burn, but the footsteps behind me make me jump up as fast as I can, and I keep running. I can't stop. I won't stop.

This is my only shot at freedom.

My life in my own hands.

I haven't felt the heat of the sun on my skin since I was in that damp cage in the compound. Haven't tasted the fresh air on my tongue or smelled the scent of burning ground in ages.

And it's invigorating.

It gives me the energy I need to fight.

To flee and run for my life.

My muscles ache, but that won't stop me from running.

I'm out of breath, but I keep going. I refuse to stop.

Not even when I fall and have to crawl back up again, multiple times.

Nothing motivates me more than the threat of pain.

Because this man … is right behind me.

And I don't know what will happen if he ever manages to catch me.

I can't let it happen.

But I can hear his growls and footsteps just as hard behind me, and they never disappear. Not even when I push myself to run so fast my legs feel like they're about to cave.

Suddenly, something latches on to my ankles, and I topple over.

"Got you …"

I squeal when he crawls on top of me. I fight, but he's much stronger than I am, and he's quickly covered my body with his, making it impossible to crawl away.

"Too slow," he says, his voice low and slick as he keeps me pinned to the ground.

"Please …" I mumble, tears welling up in my eyes.

I managed to roll onto my back when he grabbed me, but now I fear what's going to happen.

Something sharp slides along my neck. Something cold … and metallic.

Tears well up in my eyes. "Please …" I mutter again, almost choking on my own words.

"Shhh …" he whispers, his voice so soft it's like that of a demon disguised as an angel.

My whole body shivers as the blade shifts positions, carefully crafting a line down toward my chest where it stays. Pointed right at my heart.

Tears roll down my cheeks. I freeze.

Is this the end?

Is he going to kill me?

"Please, don't do this," I beg.

But there's no reply.

I wait and think about all the things I still wanted to do. Still wanted to experience. All the things I'd miss in this world.

I might not have a family or a good home to go back to, but dammit, I don't want to die.

Now, more than ever, I want … to live.

And as the blade pushes into my skin, I await my fate, knowing it wasn't my choice. I fought, I ran, I failed, but I never gave up. That must be worth something.

Seconds feel like minutes as he holds me to the ground.

Maybe it actually has been minutes. I can't tell.

All I feel is the sharp point against my body.

And then wetness ... drip. Drip.

Onto my chest.

Motionlessly, I lie underneath him as his grip on me begins to fade in strength.

The blade slowly pulls away until I no longer feel it on my skin.

Is this a trick? Is he just messing with me? Trying to get me to face my own death with dignity?

I wait in shock, my body not even responding to the fact that he's no longer holding me down.

Still, wetness drips onto my skin.

Is he ... crying?

Something clatters to the ground. The metal clashing with the rocks.

I suck in a breath.

Suddenly, he has his arms around my back, and he lifts me up from the ground. Pulls me close. Into his embrace.

My lips part. "Wha—"

"I can't ... oh God, does it mean that I ..." he murmurs into my ears, not finishing his sentence.

As my own salty tears enter my mouth, I just sit there and accept his comforting hug.

I don't know what else to do.

Nothing makes sense.

"I'm sorry ..." he murmurs. "I'm so sorry."

My brain is spinning, overgrown with thoughts of murder. Of how the blade was about to pierce my skin. How, at this very moment, he could still be reaching for the blade to thrust it into me.

Maybe it's all a ruse.

Maybe it's all lies meant to make me feel safe, even when I'm not.

But then he does the most peculiar thing.

He whispers into my ear, "Thank you."

THREE

CHASE

I feel elated and vicious at the same time.

Two emotions that can't be more of a duality.

Yet they co-exist inside me ... peacefully.

I was right.

This moment ... it was *everything*.

A spectacle.

A magnificent, thundering explosion of clashing thoughts and needs.

It was all my doing ... and now, it's finally finished.

For a split second, I wonder what made it final. Was it her eyes? Her shivering body curled underneath mine? Her tears that kept flowing? Her sweet voice as she begged me to let her live?

Or maybe it was a culmination of all those things.

In any case, what's done is done. Time can't be turned back. The decision is final.

I know the truth now.

Still, I can't stop holding her tight. I wish I never had to let go, but I know that moment has to come sometime. She won't accept this for much longer.

So I take a deep breath and push her back. I smile, knowing what this means.

It's done. It's finally over.

I don't know who won, but it doesn't matter.

All that's left now is to pick up the pieces and move on.

However, the moment I release her, her body slumps and falls to the ground. Did she faint because of the stress? She must have.

I quickly grasp her body and pull her toward me, so I can cradle her as I get up from the ground.

I carry her back all the way to the car where a sullen looking Brandon sits behind the wheel, waiting for me.

"Don't," I say when he opens his mouth. "I don't want to hear it."

The left side of his lips tips up as he shakes his head. "I can't believe it. Really?"

"Like I said … it doesn't matter. I know now." I open the door and lay her down on the back seat. After I attach the seat belt, I bind her wrists and ankles with a few zip ties so she can't break the windows when she wakes up. Then I get into the passenger's seat and buckle up.

"And what's next? What are you gonna do now, huh?" he asks, gripping the steering wheel casually with his hands.

I lick my lips and stare out into the sunset. It marks the beginning of a new chapter in my life ... and hers. "Now, we go home."

***

When we get to my place, she's already awakened. She hasn't spoken a word since we were still in the canyon, after I chased her and caught her. Her last words were pleas, but when I turn and look at her now, all I see is rage. Her whole body is tense, and she refuses to unclench her jaws.

I know she's angry. She has every right to be.

Brandon drives the car into the parking lot while I take off the zip ties around her ankles and escort her to my home. She comes willingly, without a fuss. I don't know why she's not putting up much of a fight like she did before the chase.

It's as if she's lost a bit of the spark she had.

Like the knife ... siphoned it out of her.

Made her meek and fearful.

I can tell when I bring her into a room. *Her* room.

The moment I release her, she immediately scurries to a corner as far away from me as she possibly can, where she sits down and pretends she doesn't exist.

Frowning, I clutch the door and sigh.

I know what I've caused. It had to be done ... but it came at a hefty price.

Her misery isn't something I enjoy. Even though she'd probably never believe me if I told her.

I close the door and turn on the light. It only helps me, not her. She still shivers as I approach her slowly, trying not to scare her. I lean down in front of her and touch her skin. It's soft and warm. But she immediately leans away, turning her head.

She doesn't want my affection.

Of course not.

What am I thinking?

I let out another sigh and lower my head, closing my eyes.

I wish I could take her pain away, but I can't. I *caused* it.

"I'm sorry," I say, my voice softer than before. "That will never happen again."

Her jaw clenches, but she doesn't say a word. Even though I expected her to. Is she that scared of me?

Dammit.

If she hates me this much already, there's no telling what she'll do if she gets out of her bonds.

What if she lashes out? Or escapes? Or worse ... reports me for doing all the things I did?

It would ruin me.

She may not have seen my face, but she knows my name. And she may be skilled enough to lead the police back to my home.

I can't let it happen.

So I quickly get up and rummage through the drawer until I find what I'm looking for. A chain and collar ... once used by one of the girls I had in my home who insisted on being my pet. I got rid of her the moment she started snooping around, but I kept the gear. I knew it might be useful one day ... and I was right.

I lower myself to her level again and slide aside her hair. Her skin feels so soft and warm. Unlike mine.

She's shivering as the collar locks into place.

I tuck the key into my pocket and stare at her for a few seconds.

She still hasn't moved from her spot.

Hasn't even responded to the fact that I collared her ... and that I chained her to the bed.

I lean forward, tempted to remove it, but I stop myself before I do.

I can't give in this easily.

I know it's wrong, but what else can I do? The zip ties won't last, and she'll surely try to escape. Who knows what kind of trouble she might give me if she finds a way to get out.

She might be blind, but I know she has more guts than this. I could see it in the way she ran, how she fled for her life. She has spirit.

"What ... what are you going to do with me?" she asks as I get up and walk away.

I stop in my tracks and glance at her over my shoulder.

She's so beautiful. Too beautiful.

And I ruined it.

I ruined that pretty face. Stained it with tears that were not supposed to be there.

And for what? My own selfish needs.

I shake my head and rub my forehead. "I don't ... know yet."

Then I quickly open the door and slam it shut before I say anything more stupid than what just came out of my mouth.

For a moment, I just stand there, overwhelmed by my own emotions.

I feel sick.

I *never* feel sick.

At least not like this.

Like I want to strangle myself. Slam myself into a window and just be done with it.

I need to get this need out of me. Need to rinse myself of the evil that's settled in my blood.

Brandon is standing in the kitchen, casually sipping coffee and glaring at me from the corner of his eyes with that familiar look. That look that says *I know what you're thinking.*

I hate that he knows me so well.

I cross my arms and raise a brow at him. "What?"

"Nothing."

I roll my eyes. "Right."

"Want some coffee?" he asks. "You look like you could

use some."

"No thanks," I say, waving it away.

"So what are you going to do with her?" he asks.

Of course, he wants to know. He's been dying to know ever since we got back to the car and drove home. The question has been lying on the tip of his tongue all this time, and now he's finally found the right time to throw it out there.

Except I don't know the fucking answer.

I sigh and walk to the kitchen too, pouring myself a glass of water, gulping it down in one go. "I'll figure it out."

I place it down on the countertop and grab my coat again.

"So what now? You're just gonna leave her in there?"

"Yep," I say, putting on my coat.

"Where are you going?"

I narrow my eyes. "Do you really have to ask?"

He puts down his cup. "Really? You're gonna do that *now?*"

"Yes. I need to blow off some steam."

"I thought you said you were done," he says, following me to the door.

"No, I said I knew the truth now. I never said anything about being done forever."

"What do you want me to do now?"

"Look after her," I reply.

"What? No. You brought her back here. She's your responsibility."

I glance over my shoulder and growl, "I'm asking you politely, Brandon … do this for me."

He swallows and takes a deep breath. "Fine. But don't think I'm gonna clean up after you."

Before he can say another word, I close the door behind me.

***

Syrena

Staring in the direction of the door, I sit and wait. With my hands bound, I can't attempt to escape until my captor frees me. While I wait, all I can do is stand up and sit down. All while touching that … *thing* around my neck.

The metal feels cold but not too tight.

But I know what it is.

A collar.

I can feel the chain attached to it, and I already followed it all the way back to the origin. The ring at the foot of the bed. I've jerked it and twisted it with my mouth, but nothing I did could break it. So I directed my attention to another problem I need to solve.

Breaking out of here.

I've already tried using my teeth to open the windows

and doors, but no luck. They're tightly locked, and I presume they can't be opened from the inside.

Which makes me wonder … is it on purpose? Did he always intend to keep someone here?

It must be … why else would he have this collar on hand?

Unless he was expecting me.

Or is this all just a coincidence?

Not that there's any use thinking about things you can't change.

I'm here; he's out there. End of story.

I still wonder who he is, though, and what he wants from me. Why he chained me up and put zip ties around my wrists.

If there's anything I know … there's one thing men want most of all. And if that's the case, will I be prepared for that, just so I can escape? Will he let me go if I give him what he wants?

Or do I have to fight?

Then again, the world out there is a cruel one, and the longer I think about it, the less I actually want to go back. No one would call the place I used to live in a proper home.

No, I promised myself back when I was still imprisoned in a cage by Graham that I would start a new life once I got out of there. One where I don't have to service men and do their dirty work. One where I can just be … at peace.

I sigh and sit back down on the floor in the middle of the room again.

Right as I do, the door unlocks and then creaks. I suck in a breath and wait until the footsteps are audible. Then I slowly slide backward until my back hits the wall.

"Don't be afraid …"

It's a different voice. Not him.

Must be that Brandon guy.

It's quiet for some time before he speaks up again. "The collar? Okay …"

He sounds surprised.

Strange.

"What do you want?" I ask.

"Nothing. I just came to check on you," he says. His voice is much less commanding than Chase's. "I brought you something to drink."

I lean back as he approaches me, and I'm hesitant to even acknowledge his existence at this point. It could put me in more danger, and I don't know what their end goal is. Why they're keeping me.

All I know is that Chase … tried to kill me.

And then he *didn't*.

Why?

It doesn't make any sense.

He cried, and then he just hugged me.

He went from a calm and collected murderer to an erratic caregiver in a split second. What does it mean?

If only I could ask him myself. Then again, I might not get an answer I like.

But he did say he was sorry. I wonder why he felt the

need to say it. It made me feel a little less ... hunted.

"Here," Brandon says, breaking my train of thought.

I don't know what he's trying to give to me, and I'm not sure I want to know.

"It's tea," he adds.

I still don't reply.

"Oh," he mumbles. "Right. He tied your hands." He clears his throat. "Well, I can put it against your lips and then you can drink."

When he does, the searing heat of the mug makes me hiss.

"Sorry," he says, immediately pulling it away. "I guess that was stupid of me."

As he gets up again, I say, "Wait." When there's no response, I add, "I'm thirsty."

"I'll get you some water instead."

The door creaks and then closes, and I'm alone again. I've never felt so much solitude as I do now. The cage was different. I shared it with people ... with Cage and Ella.

God. Just thinking about them makes me tear up.

Graham pulled me away from them, and I never even got to say goodbye.

How are they doing now? Are they still alive? What's going to happen to them?

I wish I could send them something, anything, to let them know I'm okay.

At least, for now.

The door opens again, and my whole body tenses as

Brandon sits down in front of me. "Here."

A glass is placed against my lips, this time cold, and I let it sit there for a while even though he's urging me to drink.

"Don't worry … it's not poisoned," he says, laughing. "If we wanted to kill you, we would have. Trust me."

How comforting. Not.

Still, I take a sip. The cold liquid feels too good not to. I'm so fucking thirsty that I gulp it down until the last drop.

"I'll get you some more soon," he says, and I can hear a hint of a smile as he blows out his breath. "Anyway, since you're blind, I just wanted to let you know … there's a bed to your right and a toilet to your far left. In case you need to use them."

Interesting, but nothing I couldn't have found out on my own. I don't know what he wants from me. Does he want me to thank him? Fuck that.

It's quiet for some time. Neither of us speak. I don't know if I can trust him or Chase.

Anything I say can be used against me.

I'm a prisoner in a home of a man I don't know, and nothing will stop him from doing whatever he wants to me.

I can't make it easy for them.

"You don't have to worry," Brandon says, placing a hand on my knee.

I inch back, afraid.

"Don't be scared. We won't hurt you."

"He already did," I utter, barely able to say it because I'm choking up again.

"I know," he says. "That's why he's left for now."

Left us? Chase is gone?

"He needed to cool down."

From what? Buying me? Hunting me? Keeping me?

Or all the above?

"But I know he'll take good care of you," he says.

"Who are you people, and what do you want from me?" I can't stop myself. The words just spill out of me.

I can hear him smile again. The glass is placed on the floor. "Call me Brandon. I help out Chase sometimes with things that are ... difficult."

Difficult. Does he mean me?

"Why?"

"He and I go back a long time." He snorts. "But anyway, what I want to say is ... I don't want anything from you, and I promise you I won't hurt you," he says. "But I want you to be careful around Chase."

I suck in a breath.

Did he just tell me to be wary of his partner?

Are they even partners?

"He has a ... temper that can get out of hand quickly."

"And you?" I mumble.

"You don't need to worry about me. I won't be here long."

Why? Where is he going?

"I just want to say ... Chase isn't a bad man. I know he won't hurt you. If you do what he says."

"I'm not someone's puppet," I growl back.

I don't know where I find the sudden courage to speak up.

"I know. That's why he ... bought you," he says. "To save you."

I struggle not to snort. I doubt that's true.

"He attacked me. With a knife," I say, swallowing away the lump in my throat.

It's quiet for a second.

"I know."

A shiver runs up and down my spine.

The air in the room moves as he gets up and walks away.

When the door closes, I know he's gone.

FOUR

CHASE

It's already midnight by the time I get home.

I took my sweet-ass time. A necessary evil.

When I close the door behind me, the silence in the room is irrefutable ... even though I'm not the only one here.

Brandon is sitting on the windowsill, staring out into the empty darkness. A full cup of coffee sits next to him, but it's no longer steaming, so I bet it's gone cold.

He doesn't even look at me as I walk to the kitchen and turn on the faucet. I stick my hands underneath and wash off the red, watching it disappear down the drain. My clothes seem fine, luckily. I'd hate to see them ruined. But I took measures beforehand.

I dry my hands, still holding the towel as I walk toward Brandon. He's turned around now, and he picks up the cup to take a quick sip, only to pull a sour face. Then he pours the coffee into the plant beside him.

"Really?" I raise a brow.

"Feel better?" Brandon asks, completely ignoring what he just did.

I nod.

"Good." He gets up and brings the mug to the kitchen, passing me by as if it means nothing.

But we both know that isn't true.

He knows exactly what it meant to me ... what it does to *us*.

We're both chained to the same desires.

The same sin.

He's right. I feel much better. Like the calm after the storm.

But I can tell it only worsened his mood.

"Couldn't you have waited?" he asks.

"No, and you know damn well why."

"By helping you out, I was under the impression that'd be the end of things."

"I only wanted to know the real me," I say. "And you know damn well that was the *only* reason."

"But she's still *alive*," he says. "This wasn't how it was supposed to go."

"Yes. I fucking know that."

"And now what? What are you gonna do with her?"

"I'm not done yet. I need to know how far I can take this. How far I can go."

His face darkens. "I'm not okay with you doing this. You know that."

"Oh yeah, I know." I shake my head and rub my forehead.

"Right." He scoffs. "I'm off."

I swallow back the annoyance. "Home or …?"

"You know."

His crabby response is enough. He's right. I know damn well how it feels.

We're both at the end of our wits today.

Nothing makes sense anymore.

I thought I knew what I'd want, what I'd do … once I knew the truth.

But I don't.

I know less than before I even started this.

"See ya," Brandon says with a mellow voice, and he closes the door behind him, leaving me alone with my thoughts. And *her*.

I take a sip of water from the faucet before drying my mouth with my hand.

It's time … It's time to face her.

***

Syrena

When the door creaks open, I inch back until I'm against the wall again and clench my legs together.

I don't know who it is or why he's here, but making myself tiny makes me feel safer.

Hours have passed, and in that time, I've regained a little of my strength and my voice.

I don't want to be afraid anymore. But I also don't want to give him a reason to hurt me.

I don't know what these men are capable of … yet.

All I know is that one of them tried to kill me. I have to keep that in mind, always.

The door closes, and a light switch is flipped. Not that I can see, but I can hear.

Some people view me as weak when they find out I'm blind. But the sensitivity of all my other senses has increased to compensate for my lack of sight. My ears work better than anyone else's, just like my nose. I can tell people apart just by sniffing them. And I can tell a person and if they're mad or happy just by his or her footsteps.

And judging from the sound he makes … it's definitely Chase.

My tongue dips out to wet my lips.

Why did he come into this room?

He's getting closer and closer.

Then ... a small breath on my cheeks.

"Don't be afraid," he says.

He's right in front of me and on my level.

His thumb brushes along my chin, making me look up. He wants to see me. But why? Why does he care how I look if all he wants is to use me and keep me like some pet?

Is that what this is?

His finger brushes along my lips, and my teeth lurch out to bite him instinctively. I don't think about it. I just do it.

He flinches, leans back, hisses. Sucks his finger. I can hear his tongue wrap around it. It's a delicate sound. Shiver-inducing.

But what I did will surely piss him off. I brace for impact, expecting a smack to the face anytime now.

However, nothing happens.

But he's still there. I can feel it in the air.

And he sighs.

"You won't ... hurt me?" I ask, curious as to why he would suddenly be so apprehensive, when he'd attacked me before.

"No," he says, swallowing. "I promise."

His voice sounds less dark than before. Much more ... relaxed.

Like some kind of load was lifted off his shoulders.

But the longer he stays, the more the questions seep back into my mind. And now that I'm sure he's no longer trying to kill me ... I feel safer to ask them.

"Why did you buy me?"

It takes him a while to answer. He sucks in a deep breath first. "Actually ... I don't know anymore."

What kind of answer is that?

"But I want to find out."

It doesn't make any sense. He seemed so clear about his reasons before. So commanding and in control. And now? His voice is erratic, uncertain. As if he's not even sure about himself anymore.

What does it mean?

"Here," he mumbles. After a few seconds, a hot spoon presses against my lips. "I brought you some vegetable soup. Thought you might be hungry."

For a few seconds, I contemplate it, but then my stomach growls. I can hear him smile, which means he heard it too. Dammit.

I don't want to admit that I'm hungry, but I've been famished all day. I can't say no to food that smells so good.

So I open my mouth and let him push the spoon in slowly, not too far, until the warm liquid is on my tongue, and I swallow it.

It tastes divine. Much better than anything I had at the compound. Graham was never a great cook. But this? This is ... Jesus, so good.

It almost makes me tear up. Dammit, I don't want him to see me cry. Not again.

But he keeps feeding me diligently, putting the utmost care into each spoonful that he puts into my mouth like he wants me well fed. As if he wants to satisfy my cravings and fill me up so I won't go hungry.

Like he actually cares.

Graham never treated me like that.

For the first time in a long time, I don't feel like the trash left outside next to the garbage bin.

I actually feel like a normal human being.

***

CHASE

I continue feeding her until the entire bowl is empty. As I scrape the bottom of the bowl, I feel a pang of guilt stinging in my side. Maybe I should've brought more. I'll get her some bread and butter next time. And maybe I can cook a nice meal. I have many recipes at my disposal, and I love working in the kitchen.

It puts my mind at ease.

But looking at her now while she licks her lips unwinds something inside me I didn't even know existed in the first place. And I can't help myself from reaching for her face and caressing her cheek softly. For a second there, it almost feels as though she leans into my hand.

But then her jaw tenses, and the moment fades.

I pull back.

None of this is right.

I'm keeping her locked up in a room with a chain around her neck like a goddamn dog.

Just so she won't escape and rat me out.

Fuck. What have I done?

The bowl drops from my hand.

Without looking twice, I get up and march out the door, slamming it shut behind me.

I can't think like this. What's done is done. I can't turn back time. I've made my choice, and now I have to stick with it.

But damn ... why does it have to be so goddamn difficult?

I never expected her to be so ... alluring.

Every time I step into the room and see those gorgeous translucent eyes and that soft skin of hers, it tugs at my heartstrings. She's ... someone different. Someone I never expected. Someone I've never experienced in my life before.

I felt it the moment I saw her cry in the canyon, and I never stopped feeling it whenever I look at her.

I'm overcome with guilt that I can't seem to escape, no matter how hard I try to ignore it.

My fists clench.

I have to fight it. For my own good. This is all for a greater good.

Keeping her here could still serve a purpose.

Even if I passed the first test, it doesn't mean I won't fail soon.

I have to see how far I can take it. How far I can go.

We can't leave any stone unturned.

See no evil. Hear no evil. Speak no evil.

God will be the one to judge.

I nod to myself and march into my bathroom where I strip off all my clothes and turn on the shower. I step under and let the water wash away my sins like it always does.

Except these recent marks ... aren't on my skin.

They're carved into my soul.

But the longer I stand here with water cascading down my back, the more I succumb to my own thoughts. Memories. Scents.

God ... she smelled so fucking nice.

When I touched her, I almost wanted to grab a strand of her hair and bring it to my nose for another whiff. The only thing that stopped me was the tenseness in her muscles.

She's still afraid of me ... and she has every right to be.

I wish I could take that fear away, but how?

Should I feed her more? Give her attention? Talk with her?

Taking off her collar would be the first thing on that list. But that's where my hesitance steps in.

I don't want her to run. Would she run if I took off the chain? Maybe.

I don't know, and I doubt she'd give me an honest answer.

I sigh and rest my head against the wall as I soak in the water.

The least I can do is try. I have to start somewhere.

I need to treat her better. Give her everything she needs. Anything she wants.

Maybe ... just maybe ... she could be the one to undo me.

The one to keep me in check.

A smile slowly spreads across my lips.

Yes.

She will make me a better man.

FIVE

Syrena

Hours pass before I hear another sound.

He must be awake.

I yawn and rub my face against my shoulder, forcing myself to wake up.

I barely closed my eyes last night. Even though the bed was comfy, I couldn't sleep, preferring to sit on the floor. It made me feel grounded. Safe.

But it hasn't done my brain any good. I'm so goddamn sleepy that my eyes are droopy, and it's hard to stay awake … but I have to be alert when he comes in to the room.

When the door creaks again, my muscles go rigid.

I wait.

In he steps.

He closes the door behind him and makes his way toward me. I can smell milk and something else ... something sweet.

"I brought you some cereal and a bagel," he says with a soft voice that almost sounds kind.

I swallow back the saliva as he brings it up to my nose, and the scents drift into my nostrils.

"Go on ... take a bite," he says.

And I do. God, I'd fucking do whatever he wants me to if I could have it all. I haven't had good food in such a long time; it makes me moan a little.

He snorts.

Shit.

I chew slower and try not to make a sound while swallowing. I'm embarrassed, though it was definitely worth it just to taste that bagel.

When it's gone, he pushes a spoonful of milk and cereal against my mouth, and I gleefully take a bite.

"Like that?" he asks.

I nod slowly as I chew.

"Good. I wasn't sure what kind of foods you'd like or if you had any allergies, so I just went with the regular stuff. But if you have a preference, let me know, and I'll see what I can do."

I swallow it down. "Why?" The question slips out of my mouth.

"Because I want to take care of you."

Why does he even care so much?

What happened to the man who chased me, and who is this?

Does he have two personalities?

"I don't understand," I mutter.

"I want you to be happy, I suppose," he replies, shoving another spoonful of cereal into my mouth.

Is that why he's feeding me?

But it makes no sense. He's keeping me locked up in a room. That's not making someone happy. I'm a prisoner in his home.

When he tries to push another spoon in, I pull away and frown. "You tried to kill me … didn't you?"

He sighs, and I hear the spoon fall into the bowl.

"I can't deny that."

I suck in a breath.

"But I'm a changed man now."

"Why? What did I ever do to you?" I ask.

"Nothing. That's the exact reason I chose you."

I don't understand any of it.

"Doesn't matter. You'll understand … someday," he mumbles as if he's overthinking things when it should be easy.

Suddenly, a hand grabs my knee. I stiffen while he caresses me softly. Not sexually … just … nice. "Don't worry. You don't have to be afraid of me anymore. I promise."

"How can I trust you?" I ask.

"I'm feeding you now. Isn't that a sign of good faith?" he says, and his hand lifts from my knee. The spoon moves again.

"But …"

The spoon rests against my lips again. "Eat."

Even though I hate it, I do because I'm hungry. I need the food to sustain myself.

Still, it doesn't mean I can suddenly trust him.

It'll take much more than that from a man who pushed a knife into my skin.

When the bowl is empty, he places it somewhere. Then he grabs my chin and turns my head toward him. "You have … beautiful eyes."

"Th-thank you." I don't even know why I say thank you. Part of me wants to spit in his face right now, but that'll put my well-being in jeopardy. I have to be smart.

That … and his voice when he said it made me blush.

"Do you want to go home?"

What?

The sudden question makes my heart skip a beat.

"I …" I don't even know what I want. "Home … isn't a place I know. I don't have one."

It takes him a few seconds to respond. "You don't have a home to return to?"

I shake my head.

"Where did you sleep before Graham got to you?"

"Above Roy's Strip Club."

"Strip club?" His jaw clenches. I can hear it when he speaks.

"I worked there as a server and cleaned up after hours in exchange for a place to stay."

"Oh." It sounds as though he's drifted off into his thoughts. "Was the owner ... good to you?"

I shake my head and bite my lip. "He ... put his hands on me sometimes." I run my fingers over a scar on my shoulder. "I got this after he pushed me, and I fell into a glass table. Had to clean it up afterward too," I say. "Sometimes, he'd make me dance in front of a crowd just so he could earn a bit more cash. Said I needed to earn my stay because I was useless."

Chase growls. He actually growls, without saying a word.

Then everything goes quiet. For so long that I wonder if he's still here.

"How did Graham treat you?" he asks suddenly.

I swallow away the lump in my throat. "He made me dance until my feet bled."

"Damn ..." he says through gritted teeth. When I wait, he adds, "Continue."

"We had a tiny living space. No fresh air. Although we did have a shower and a bed, which was more than I had in the second cage. Still, I didn't see the outside for months. And he didn't feed us enough."

"Us?" he mutters. "You weren't alone in the cage?"

"I had ... friends." Just thinking about Cage and Ella makes me choke up.

I wonder how they're doing.

"He made them do ... *things* together."

"I see ..." he mumbles, but I can't gage his feelings from his reaction, which is odd.

I'm almost always able to hear what someone feels just by listening to their voice.

But with Chase, it's as if he's concealing a part of himself.

"Do you miss them?" he asks.

I nod. "Very much. They ... they don't even know if I'm alive." Tears well in my eyes again, but I push them away.

He takes a deep breath before replying. "Would you like to send them a message?"

"What?" My jaw drops.

I can't believe what he just suggested. Is this real?

"Right now, I can't get them out of there. But I can send Graham a picture of you and tell him to give it to them, so they'll know you're still alive. Just tell me what to write."

"You'd ... do that for me?" I'm completely stunned.

"Yeah. Just think about it for a while." He caresses my cheek again and wipes away a tear that managed to escape. Damn. I didn't want him to see me cry, but the thought of sending them something, anything, fills me with hope ... which is something I haven't felt in such a long time.

"I won't make you do anything you don't want to," he says, his voice dark but laced with regret. "Understand?"

I nod softly.

His fingers leave my face. "I'm bad, Syrena. You should know that."

"But—"

Suddenly, he grabs my shoulders and says, "Call me a monster. Say it to my face."

"What?" I mutter, surprised by the sudden change of his character.

"Say it!" he yells.

"You're ... a monster," I say, confused as fuck.

The shaking stops, but his hands are still clutching my shoulders, his nails digging into me.

"You're hurting me," I say.

He immediately releases me.

"I'm sorry," he says, and he gets up from the floor. "I shouldn't have."

As he stomps off, I call out. "Wait!"

His footsteps stop.

"Will I ever ... be allowed out?" I ask.

He sighs softly. "Maybe. If you promise you won't escape."

No matter how hard I try, my mouth doesn't open. My lips refuse to utter the words.

So he walks out and closes the door behind him.

Shit.

***

CHASE

Fuck.

I felt so bad for putting her through all that.

I had to get out of there before I succumbed. Before …

Fuck.

Every time I see her face, I just want to hug her. And those lips as she gulps down the food are … goddamn sinful.

I can't stop thinking about prying them open with my tongue.

No.

That's the last thing I should be thinking about right now.

She hates me, and she should. I did something horrible to her. She deserves better than this.

But fuck, I need her.

I need her more than she knows.

If I'd known she was in such a terrible place, that Graham was treating her so badly, I would've gotten her out much sooner.

I would've gone over to Graham's and pulled her out without question. I don't even care how much I'd need to pay just to have her … and her friends, for that matter.

Shit.

I run my fingers through my hair and pace up and down

the hallway.

I knew he was fucked up for keeping them locked in cages, but I thought he was only selling them to others. I didn't know he was using some of them for himself too. That changes the entire game.

Did he use Syrena too?

Did he touch her the way I can only dream of touching her?

"Fuck!"

The moment I pass the mirror, I stop in my tracks and stare myself down.

Fuck this man staring right back at me.

Fuck this man who doesn't know wrong from right.

Fuck this man who did the unthinkable …

Just fuck.

In an instant, my fist slams into the mirror, smashing it to pieces.

Glass flies everywhere, littering the floor.

Some shards pierce my hand.

I stretch out my fingers and watch the blood run down my hand. Damn. That hurt. But it felt so good too.

Shaking the remnants of glass from my hand, I grab my cell phone and call Brandon.

"Hey. Have some new names on the list?" I hiss.

"Hi to you too. Yeah, I have some."

"Just get me a name. Anything. I don't care. I need to get my fix."

"What? Already?"

"Yes, *now*," I growl.

"Geez, all right, dude. Calm down," he says.

"No, I'm not fucking calm," I say, glaring at my bloody fingers. "I just broke a fucking mirror because she's here."

"Then get rid of her."

"Stop fucking suggesting the impossible!" I yell. "You know I need her, and you know damn well why."

"Guess it isn't working as well as you hoped then. Also, I'm pretty sure she can hear you now."

"I don't fucking care! Get me a name. I'll take care of it on my own."

Sometimes, I really regret leaving the list to him. Maybe I should start keeping my own again.

Before he can throw me another witty remark, I hang up.

He knows just as well as I do how bad shit can get when I'm this agitated.

And he doesn't want me on his bad side.

That, I'm sure of.

SIX

Syrena

Later that night, he comes into my room with more food.

It smells delicious. Something with meat and veggies.

"Brought you a stew."

"It smells good," I say.

I know I shouldn't be nice to him but playing along might be the better thing for me to do if I want to survive.

He sits down in front of me and feeds me once again, just like before. Now that he's done it a couple of times, I'm more aware of when he's going to push a spoon or a fork into my mouth, and I actually start to anticipate it.

The meal tastes delicious, and I can't help but chow down eagerly, awaiting the next bite.

Him feeding me like this ... it reminds me of a drug addiction.

You hate it, but you don't want it to stop.

That's how I feel right now.

"All gone," he says, smiling right after. "You sure were hungry."

"Sorry," I say, shrugging. "I just like food a lot."

He laughs. "I can tell."

I lick my lips to get the last bit of juicy sauce off, but then his finger circles around my collar, pulling me closer.

I hold my breath as his face is inches away from mine. I can tell from his breath scattering on my skin.

"If I take this off ... will you stay?"

I don't know how to respond. All I can do is nod.

"Promise me."

Why does he care so much?

"But you ... wanted to kill me," I mutter.

"I don't want you dead," he says. "Please, believe me when I say I *never* wanted you dead."

"Then why did you attack me?" I ask.

He sighs, and I can hear the strain in his voice. "Because ... it's who I am." His finger releases the band around my neck, but he grabs the chain instead, holding me close. "Please. Just ... promise me you won't escape."

Is it a threat?

Will he hurt me if I try?

Possibly.

But taking off this collar and being freed from this single room is better than being chained up. If it means I'll have to promise him something, then so be it.

"Okay," I reply.

He places both hands on my cheeks, and I can sense his closeness. For some reason ... his touch makes my face tingle.

Shit.

"Thank you," he says.

Soon after, the collar around my neck clicks and releases. Then he takes off the zip ties from my wrists.

I'm free.

My hands instantly go to my neck. Touching myself to make sure I'm still okay. I don't feel pain. There are no wounds.

I breathe a sigh of relief.

"Now, if you behave, I'll let you roam free in my house. Understood?"

I nod.

I don't know why I'm so complacent. I normally never am. This isn't me.

But something about his voice just makes me ... weak.

Fuck.

He gets up and then grabs my hand, pulling me up too. But because I've been sitting for so long, I feel dizzy, and I collapse ... right into his arms.

"Easy," he mumbles, his voice much sweeter than

before.

What is this? Why is he so nice all of the sudden?

I don't understand this man, yet he's petting me as if I'm a kid he needs to take care of.

I push myself away from him and say, "I'm not weak."

"I never said you were," he says, and he snorts.

I take a deep breath and listen to the sounds around me, waiting for him to say what he wants me to do. There must be some reason he's keeping me here.

Still, if I'm going to be cooped up in a man's house like some pet, I'd like to know who he is. What he looks like. Or at least ... get familiar with him so I don't have to be scared anymore.

He grabs my hand again, but when I don't follow him, he says, "You can trust me."

I frown. He says it like it's the truth, but how would I know? All I know is the man keeping me locked up in a room after attempting to take my life in the desert. Trust isn't exactly the easiest follow-up.

But if he wanted to kill me, he would've done it already. Right?

That must mean something.

"Come," he says, trying to pull me along again, but I hesitate.

"Wait."

He stops.

"I ..." God, why is this so hard to ask? "Can I ... feel your face?"

"Why?"

"So I know what you look like," I answer.

Slowly but gently, he lifts my hand and brings it to his face, where he lets it go. I suck in a breath and start feeling around. Running my thumbs along his nose, his ears, his sharp jaw and pronounced chin, the stubble all around his mouth, his pronounced but thin lips, and the thick brows lining his eyes. His hair runs back along his head, slick and gelled all the way down his neck.

And for some reason, my hands don't stop there.

They go down his neck and along his shoulders to his chest ... and I feel every inch of thick muscle underneath the button-up shirt he's wearing. His nipples peak. I swallow as heat spreads across my cheeks.

"Felt enough?" he asks, pulling me from my thoughts.

Fuck. What am I even doing?

I immediately take my hands off him.

That was awkward.

"Yeah ... thanks," I reply.

He immediately grabs my hand again and pulls me along. "Come. I'll show you around."

My feet traipse behind him, while I carefully count the number of steps inside this room. When the door opens, I've counted six. It's five more to the table.

"Oh, watch out," he says. "Sharp corners."

"It would be easier if you let me do this on my own," I say.

It takes him a while to release my hand.

Maybe he's scared …

Of me trying to hurt him?

Or of me hurting myself?

I'm not sure, which is why I move away from him before I do anything stupid.

I touch the chairs and shuffle across the floor until I come across the wall, which I follow all the way to a door.

"That's where your room is," he says.

"Okay."

I follow along the wall to a television, and just behind it is a small coffee table and a couch.

To the left feels like windows, and in the far corner is the kitchen, because I can open all the cabinets and drawers. Would this be where he keeps the knives?

One of them won't open, though. It's locked.

"You won't find any knives, if you're looking," he says.

Shit.

Guess he saw right through me.

Am I that easy to read? Or do we just think alike?

"I've put away anything dangerous." There's a smug sound to his voice that makes me narrow my eyes.

"How thoughtful," I reply cynically.

When I find the sink, I turn on the faucet and let the warm water run along my hands. God, it feels so good. I find the soap bottle and squirt some onto my hands, washing them until they're soft. They haven't felt this nice in ages, and I can't stop touching them after they've dried.

"Feels good?"

I jolt from the sudden closeness of his voice.

I never actually heard him walk toward me. Was I so focused on what I was doing? Or is he able to make himself unheard?

Just the thought of not being able to hear where he is makes goose bumps scatter on my skin.

"Want to take a shower?" he says.

I nod. Dying. I'm dying for a shower. But I won't admit that to him.

"Thought so. C'mon." He grabs my hand again, but this time, it feels less forceful and much more as though he's trying to guide me around his apartment. If that's what this is, because I'm not sure if there's more. But it is really, really huge. Penthouse huge. Which isn't strange, considering he spent money on an actual human being.

I know he bought me. I just don't know how much he paid for me. I couldn't hear anything when I was in that small cage during the auction, unlike the bigger glass prison where I lived before with Ella and Cage. But when I was taken away and put there ... it felt like I was put on display for all to see.

It made me feel filthy.

Like I needed to wash something off.

"Here we are," Chase says, stopping in his tracks and releasing my hand. He flips a switch and says, "Towels are in the cabinet in the corner, next to the shower. Sink is right beside you. Shower is in the back. And there's a tub to your left. That's about it."

"Thanks," I say.

I'm dying to get rid of these panties and this bra Graham made me wear when he imprisoned me. But Chase is still here, and I'm very much aware of his presence.

Of course, he won't leave.

I might try to escape … or worse, harm him.

Or maybe he thinks I might harm myself.

None of that is true. I just want to take a shower. And right now, I don't care if he watches me or not.

***

CHASE

"Go ahead. I won't look," I say.

She shrugs and hooks her fingers underneath the band of her bra to unclip it. "I don't mind. I'm blind, so I won't know anyway," she replies.

A smirk spreads across my lips. I like her already.

I almost can't believe she said that. Then again, Graham already said she was the sassiest of all three. I'm going to have my hands full with her.

Both figuratively … and literally.

Because fuck me … I can't stop myself from peeking as her bra drops to the floor, and two magnificent tits fall out. Plump and juicy … ready to be sucked until her nipples peak.

Fuck.

Why am I even thinking this?

I shake my head and force myself to forget that image.

However, when I open my eyes again, she's turned her head toward me, almost as if she can sense I did something ... or *thought* something dirty.

Guess we're more in tune than I thought.

Her fingers curl around her panties, and she pulls them down, just like that. Not giving a shit that I'm here. Watching.

As she said, she can't see, so how would she know?

Still, I feel like a goddamn pervert, so I avert my eyes as she steps underneath the showerhead and turns on the water. But no matter how hard I try, I can't get that perfect round butt out of my mind. Or how badly I want to bite it.

Fuck.

What the hell is wrong with me?

I can't think these things. Not with her.

It's wrong. It's sinful. And it makes me the fucking devil.

So I immediately turn around and close the door behind me, breathing in and out to calm down. I'd intended to stay and watch, in case she decided to grab something like a razor or smash the mirror to use it as a weapon, but I can't do it.

I just can't.

I was *this* close. This close ... to just grabbing her body and fucking her right then and there.

So I slap myself.

Right in the face.

Pain is the punishment I deserve for wanting something so forbidden.

I bought her.

She's mine.

And I have to take care of what's mine.

So I walk away from the door and tell myself not to return until she calls my name.

SEVEN

Syrena

When I get out from underneath the shower, I pat myself down with the towel and wrap it around my body. Chase didn't leave any clothes. Maybe he was planning to, but he left the bathroom so suddenly I didn't have the time to ask. I guess taking my clothes off in front of him got a little too hot to handle.

I know what I have, and I'm not afraid to show it off.

Especially not if I can use it to persuade my captor.

I mean, anything goes, right?

He's keeping me a prisoner in his home, so I might as well try to get something out of it.

Maybe if I try hard enough, he'll let me go.

So I open the door and walk out into the living room. The scent of coffee hangs in the air, and I sniff to take it all in. My mouth waters as it wafts past me, out of the kitchen.

"Coffee's ready," he says.

If I remember the layout of his apartment correctly, he's already standing near the table.

"Oh …" Judging from the sound of his voice, he just looked.

My whole face turns red. "There weren't any clothes."

"Shit. I forgot." He rushes past me, into a room, but I don't know which. A few drawers open and close, and then he slams the door shut again.

"Hold out your hands." He's right in front of me now, and when I do what he asks, he puts what feels like a dress in my hands. "Put it on."

I shrug and immediately drop my towel to the floor. Then I lift my arms and slide the dress on.

I'm pretty sure he's watching.

I can tell from his hampered breaths.

I wonder if he liked what he saw.

He immediately turns and walks away. "C'mon. Sit," he says, and he pulls out a chair.

I'm still wondering why he has clothes that fit me perfectly. "This is … nice," I mumble, touching the fabric.

"You like it? I bought some on a whim. If it's not the right size, I can get you something else."

"No, it's fine," I reply, touching the table to make sure

I'm on the right side before sitting down.

"Good." He scoots my chair up and puts his hands on my shoulders, squeezing a little. "You must've missed the normal things like coffee. What else have you missed? A lot, probably," he continues. "I plan to cook for you. I want you to taste every little thing you've been missing out on for months." He leans over in my ears and says, "Do you like juicy ... red ... meat?"

"W-what?" I stammer.

"Do you like pot roast?" he asks. "Just an innocent question."

I nod, barely able to speak with his fingers digging into my skin possessively.

That didn't feel like just an innocent question.

"Good." He releases me. "I'll make it tomorrow."

He sits down across the table and grabs something. Pouring it into his coffee, he stirs loudly.

"It's right in front of you. Go ahead."

I touch the cup carefully to make sure I don't burn my hands while finding the handle. Then I bring it to my mouth and take a sip.

"No sugar? Milk?"

"I prefer it black," I reply, licking my lips from the aftertaste. God, it's been so long since I last tasted coffee. It's so good; it makes goose bumps scatter on my skin, and I actually want to moan. But I manage to stop myself before it rolls out of my mouth.

Still, I can hear him smile.

"What's so funny?" I ask.

"Nothing. I just like watching you enjoy things."

"Strange," I reply.

"How so?"

"Well, for one, you're keeping me a prisoner in your home. And two, I find that hard to believe."

It's quiet for some time before he responds. "I'm sorry, Syrena. I can't let you go."

"Why?" I ask, putting down my cup.

"What would you do if you were free? Go to the police to tell them about me."

"I wouldn't."

"Right." He takes a sip. "Who are you trying to convince?"

"I don't even know where we are. How could I ever lead them to you? I only know your first name," I reply.

"I'm not that stupid, Syrena." He scoots his chair back and gets up. The closer he walks, the more I lean back. He places one hand on the back of my chair and one on the table. "I've seen how you move around. Learning your surroundings and getting your bearings is like a snap of the finger, isn't it? You feel … you touch."

He places a hand on my shoulder and slides it down my arm. "You already know the exact layout of my home. I'm sure you could trace your way back too." He squeezes softly. A threat. "So don't lie to me … please."

I jerk free of his grip and scoot my chair back as far away from him as possible, before getting up and walking back toward the room he's been keeping me in all this time.

"Where are you going?" he asks.

"I'm tired."

"We aren't done talking."

"I am."

He growls. "Sit. Down."

"Make me," I hiss as I stampede toward the door.

Right as he stomps behind me, I slam the door shut in his face. I don't care if he comes in or not. He can't do anything to me that someone hasn't already tried. He can't take away anything I value.

He can see right through me, and I hate it.

I hate that I have nothing to persuade him with … except for my body.

Guess I will have to sell my soul.

***

CHASE

My hand hovers over the door handle, but I can't bring myself to enter. As much as I want to scream and make her do everything I want, I can't. It isn't fucking right.

Instead, I slam the wall with a fist so hard it makes my knuckles bleed.

I sink to the floor and gaze at my bloodied hand,

wondering if I can ever make this right again. If I can ever be anything less than ... bad.

I promised myself that I'd do this. That she would be the one. But she's making it so hard for me.

"Fuck!" I slam the wall again, this time with a flat hand, just to let my frustrations out.

However, it only makes them worse.

The longer I sit here steaming in my own rage, the more I want to lash out.

I have to get out. Have to get away from her. Now. Before I do something I'll forever regret.

So I get up, grab my coat, and run out the door, slamming it shut behind me.

With my cell phone in my hand, I make my way to my car and dial Brandon's number.

"I'm doing it now," I say when he picks up. "Give me an address and a name."

"Okay ... Hold on." While he's looking, I get in the car and buckle up. "I've texted you the info. Want me to come with?"

"No. I need to do this alone."

"Fine by me," he replies. "How's the girl?"

"Great."

I hang up the phone before he can say anything more about her. I know how he feels about it, but I don't fucking care whether he agrees. He knows how much this means to me, and I'm sticking with it.

I throw my phone in the passenger seat and hit the gas,

chasing the roads.

I drive just below the speed limit, never going through a red light. I hate breaking the rules, but what I hate more are rule breakers. And I will never, ever become one. Just because I'm twisted doesn't mean I'm evil.

No ... the man I'm looking at right now is.

His picture, as is his address, is on my phone when I get out of the car and open the back to take out my tools. Two black gloves, a mask that I wear, a poncho ... and an ax.

Humming a tune, I check my surroundings before stuffing the poncho and ax in a bag and closing the trunk again. Then I make my way to his home.

Harrold Magus, one of the richest men in town ... is also a fraud. His wealth came over the backs of hardworking people who he scammed out of money, then gambled it off in the stock markets. Time and time again, he got away with it, paying off the police and judges.

Not anymore.

I jump over the small fence and check my surroundings for nosy neighbors before I go to his house. It's dark inside, except for one light turned on in the bedroom. Perfect.

With a plastic card, I gain entry into his home and close the door behind me without making a sound. Slowly, I tread through the house, checking each room for people before I make my way upstairs.

Adrenaline rushes through my veins as I go up the staircase, and his shadow appears on the door.

He's right there, brushing his teeth in the bathroom.

I quietly place the bag on the floor and take out the poncho, putting it on. Then I take out the ax and approach.

My tongue dips out from excitement the closer I get.

Oh … yes. This is going to be magnificent.

One hit and he's down.

Blood sprays everywhere.

Not a sound except the smashing of his skull against the floor.

Another hit and he's surely gone forever. Smothered like a bug. Vanished from this earth like the unwanted virus he is. He won't be a fucking bloodsucker anymore.

I pull my ax from his body and clean it in the sink before putting it back in my bag along with the poncho. Then I casually stroll down the stairs, whistling that same tune from before.

The world can rest peacefully tonight.

The justice system might fail from time to time, but I won't.

I'll make sure there's justice where there's evil. No matter the price.

EIGHT

CHASE

Age sixteen

Killers aren't born. They're made.

I was always a troubled boy. But my parents never gave it a second thought. They never paid much attention to me anyway. I was a burden. Something that shouldn't have existed.

It was no wonder I eventually ended up in foster care with a mother who disappeared and a father who drank himself to death.

But bored little boys who are angry with society, angry with their parents, do things they shouldn't.

They start to punish other little boys for doing bad

things.

Pulling underwear over their head when they peed on the toilet seat.

Hitting them with a stick when they bullied others.

Giving them bloodied and broken noses when they stole candy.

I did it all and worse.

It was never enough to satiate my insane appetite for justice.

The little boy grew up, but he always kept punishing people. The older he got, the more tools he used, and the easier it became to hide behind a mask.

But nothing ever prepared him for his first murder.

When I'm in a store to buy a gift for a friend, a man comes staggering in. Grabbing a bottle of liquor, he wobbles to the cash register. But instead of paying, he pulls out a gun.

The cashier doesn't know what to do. Panics. Begins to cry.

The man threatens him. Holds him under shot.

The cashier reaches for something underneath the register. The drunken man screams.

I tackle him from behind.

We fight over the gun. In the heat of the moment, it goes off.

But instead of it aiming to kill me ... it kills him.

It takes a while for my brain to register what has happened.

But the elation and euphoria surging through my body are unmistakable.

My first kill.

And I grin ... because I already knew this would only be the beginning of something beyond this world.

Something monstrous.

Me.

***

Syrena

In the middle of the night, he comes home.

When the door closes, I slide toward the door in my room and listen to the sounds. His steps are soft but still audible.

Where the hell did he come from? And why did he come home so late?

Was it for his job? Or did he go do something else?

Curiosity gets the better of me, and I slowly open the door and listen to the sounds. He turns on the lights and water gushes out of the faucet in the bathroom.

I approach the noise and grasp the door opening.

Suddenly, metal clatters into the sink. It sounds like the soap dispenser.

"Fuck," he hisses, the water splashing everywhere, even onto my skin. "Didn't expect to see you here."

"Sorry," I say.

"I thought you were in bed."

"Couldn't sleep."

He clears his throat and continues washing something … but what?

"What are you doing?" I ask.

He sighs. "Nothing."

I sniff something in the air. A funny metallic scent, and it isn't the soap. I'm sure.

"In the middle of the night?"

"Just … go back to bed."

I frown and then grasp the thing away from him, quickly smelling it before he snags it back.

"Don't. Touch. It." Every word comes out like it's poison.

As if he's trying to scare me away.

But we already played this game, and he's not gonna win twice.

"What is it?" I ask.

"None of your business," he snaps, tucking it underneath the sink again.

"You woke me up, so now it is."

"Go to bed," he says with a stern voice.

"No. I can't sleep when you're up and about. You're washing something … clothes, maybe? And in the middle of the night even. Which begs the question …" I step closer to him. "What are you trying to hide?"

I grasp the cloth again and hold it close to my nose.

It's blood. Definitely blood.

Suddenly, he grabs my arms and shoves me against the wall. His breath mere inches away from my mouth. "I told you not to fucking touch it!"

"You're washing out blood," I reply, unshaken by his rage.

"Don't …" His voice is so low, it makes my whole body quake. But I refuse to fear him.

"Were you … hurt?" I ask.

He sucks in a breath.

His pause feels like an eternity.

Then he whispers into my ear. "Is that what you want?"

I hold my breath as his tongue dips out to lick the rim of my ear.

"No," I reply, my voice shaky.

"I don't believe you. I know you hate me," he whispers, planting one hand above me on the wall. The other snakes up my arm. "You don't have to fear me. I won't hurt you."

I don't know if I can believe him.

If he's really washing out blood, whose is it? Did he get into a fight with someone? Or is he lying to me?

A soft moan leaves his mouth, and he whispers, "It's hard to resist … So hard."

Hard to resist … *what?*

Me?

"Keep pushing me," he adds.

Is it a threat or an invitation? I can't tell.

Until he opens his mouth. "I like it."

What kind of person says that?

After being caught doing ... *this*?

"Who ... who are you?" I ask. The question just slipped out of me.

But I can't stop wondering why he's cleaning in the middle of the night. Who does that?

I can hear him smile. His hand moves up my neck ... all the way to my cheek, where he caresses me. His fingers leave a slick trail on my skin.

"Don't ask questions you don't want to know the answer to," he says. I can hear him smile. "As I said, it's none of your business. Trust me when I say you're better off not knowing."

My lips begin to tremble.

His fingers brush down my chin and then let go.

I feel like he just slid his tongue down my throat.

Like he just groped me.

Tongued me.

And I let him.

Even though none of that really happened.

It just played out in my mind.

And it's so fucked up that the moment he lifts his hand off the wall, I bolt.

***

CHASE

After washing the bloodied poncho, I dump it in the bleach and cleanse my whole bathroom. I shouldn't have brought it home with me, but tonight was an unplanned thing, and I didn't exactly have anything prepared. Guess I should've known she'd wake up from all the ruckus.

Fuck.

I slam the wall in the shower and stare down at my feet as the water pools.

How could have I been so stupid? I'm normally never this careless.

It's just that … the moment I stepped into my car again and everything was taken care of, I immediately thought of her.

Yes, right after, when adrenaline was still surging through my body, I was thinking of *her*.

And not in the gentlest of ways.

I wanted to grab her by the throat and kiss her so hard it'd steal her breath.

I wanted to fuck her brains out while she screamed out my name.

I wanted to tie her up, spank her, choke her, make her wet.

Images of sex jumbled up my brain even though I'd just committed cold-blooded murder.

This has never happened before.

Never.

And it scared the living shit out of me so much that I instantly drove back home without thinking twice.

Why? I was actually scared she already escaped, which is insane, because I locked all the doors and windows tight. There's no way out. Yet the fear was real.

Just as much as my hard-on is right now.

Fuck.

I can't stop thinking about how pretty she looked with those watery eyes, cowering between my hands, her lips plump and ripe for the taking. And how I ruined it all.

Why? Why does this have to happen?

Is this why I couldn't kill her? Because I'm infatuated with her?

If that's the case, it's all been for nothing.

It doesn't prove anything about my ability to resist evil.

Fuck!

I slam the wall again so hard that it hurts.

I let the warm water cascade down my back.

The longer she stays, the more I succumb to bad thoughts.

Her mere presence has driven me to kill. Twice now.

But I can't let her go either. There's no way out of this. I have to keep her, for as long as it takes, for as long as I need to. I don't even know why … I just know that I have to for my sake. Even though it comes at a hefty price: Her happiness.

After all the blood is gone and I'm clean, I get out from under the shower and dry off. My mind's still going in circles about what just happened and how she thought I might've been wounded. She actually thought I was the one hurt?

Or does she know now what kind of a monster I am?

She shouldn't have come in, shouldn't have touched my shit, but she couldn't ignore her curiosity.

I shouldn't have touched her, sniffed her, licked her … but God, she tasted so fucking good. But then she ran away … because of me.

Wearing nothing but a towel, I walk out of the shower and to my bedroom. I don't even go check on her because I just can't stomach seeing her face right now. I know I'm an animal. I don't need confirmation.

I throw off my towel and lie down in bed naked, staring up at the ceiling.

No matter how many times I close my eyes, I can't force myself to sleep.

Can't do anything but … think of her.

Those beautiful eyes and that sexy body I just want to fuck.

And I already know, sooner or later … it's going to happen.

Self-control isn't my best asset. It never was.

NINE

Syrena

I'm in bed, but I can't sleep.

How could anyone when they just caught someone washing out blood?

There was no mistaking it; I could smell it.

But why would he lie about it?

Why wouldn't he tell me he got into a fight?

Or is it something else he's trying to hide?

There's so much I don't understand about this man. Why he'd try to kill me one moment and then take care of me the next as if nothing ever happened. It's as if he can change his personality with the snap of a finger, and I don't know whether I should be scared or intrigued.

There's something about him ... and I want to find out what it is.

Something so much deeper than is on the surface.

But why should I? This man is keeping me a prisoner in his house.

I shouldn't even remotely care about wanting to find out who he really is, yet ... I can't stop myself from thinking about exactly that.

When we were in the bathroom, he touched me in a way he hadn't before.

Like he was ... craving me.

I felt his tongue on my ear and his fingers on my cheeks, touching me delicately as if he wanted to caress me. Make me feel wanted.

And it did, which is what scared me so much.

How does this man have so much control over me when I don't want him to? I don't even know him. He's fucking dangerous, yet I was as meek as a lamb the moment he pushed me against the wall and whispered in my ear.

My only choice was to run.

There's no way I could ever let him get close.

Right?

That's what I tell myself as I curl up in bed and wrap the blanket around me, wondering how life outside this house is moving on without me. I think about my previous home, the club, my life before the compound, and I come to the conclusion that I literally have nothing to be happy about.

Tears well up in my eyes, wishing it wasn't true.

This place—this spacious home and soft, comfortable bed, and the delectable food he cooks—can't be the best thing I've ever lived.

I refuse to believe that, because if I do ... I may never want to leave.

***

Three years ago

I hug my teddy bear for the last time before placing it back on my bed. My friends here always told me I was too old to have a teddy bear, but I don't care. It's important to me.

I don't want to leave it there because it's the only reminder I have that someone's out there waiting for me, and if I don't leave it, they'll never know I was here. They'll never be able to pick it up again and find the message tucked in the lining that says "I'm waiting for you to take me home."

If I even have any family left.

I swallow away the lump in my throat as I sigh and turn around.

I can't stay here. Despite the fact I'm not old enough to live on my own, I need to do this on my own terms. I've stayed in this orphanage for long enough. No one ever came to pick me up. No one came to take me in.

I guess that's what happens when people see a blind girl. They don't want the responsibility, the difficulties that come with that. But my blindness is not a weakness. I don't feel weak.

I march toward the windows and take out the pin from my hair. I've practiced this so many times that I know exactly which places to prod to open it.

And as I hang from the ledge and jump down on the grass, I don't stop. I don't pause to say goodbye. I just keep running ... keeping going toward a better life.

If there ever is one.

***

After months, I've finally found a place to call my own.

Well, sort of, anyway. It's a creaky old attic above the club where I work, but it's big enough for a proper bed. Plus, I have my own shower, toilet, and cooking station, which is more than I had while I lived on the streets.

I admit, life hasn't been easy since I left the orphanage, but the freedom I gained is amazing, and I wouldn't trade it for the world.

I love that I'm able to go wherever I want and do whatever I want.

The club owner, Roy, doesn't let me live here for free, so I do have to work as a server every evening. Also, it's not exactly a regular club ... more like a brothel disguised as a club. Girls are scantily dressed, and sometimes, Roy makes them dance on the makeshift stage in the back. Sometimes even half-naked and with men giving them money. I've even heard girls talk about having to suck dick and take it up the ass.

He makes me dance too sometimes. I only agreed because he demanded it, so he'd get more customers, using me as some sort of a freak show. He says it gets the men riled up.

But he doesn't have to tell me that. I know firsthand what men do when they see a girl like me dance on the stage.

They ask for more time, one-on-one time ... and I have no choice but to give in to their demands.

After all, money is money.

And Roy loves the money.

He always screams at me to do more because I live here for free. And not just that, but if I don't work hard enough, he'll smack me.

It didn't start that way. He was nice to me the first few weeks. But that all slowly changed as his health began to deteriorate, and then he started taking it out on me.

I do my best to stay positive, and I am thankful to have a place to stay, but I don't know how much longer I'll last.

As I walk along the tables and clean them, someone clears his throat in the back.

That's strange. I thought everyone had already left?

I turn and frown, listening to where the sound came from. "We're closed for the day," I say.

No response.

Maybe it was all in my head.

I shrug and continue cleaning the tables, making sure everything's ready for tomorrow, when all of the sudden there's someone shuffling behind me.

I pick up the nearest glass and hold it out in front of me like a knife.

"Who's there?"

"Relax …" His voice is low and grumbly, and it makes my skin crawl.

"Who are you? What are you doing here?"

"I'm a paying customer," the man says, chuckling.

"Please leave. We're not open," I say through gritted teeth, clenching the glass, walking backward while using the tables to guide me through the club. I have to get to the attic door. It's the only one I can lock from the inside … the only way to get away from this creep.

"You're really blind, aren't you?" he asks.

What kind of question is that?

Another pause. "I had my doubts for a few minutes, but watching you stumble around like that makes it obvious."

For a second, I stay put.

That's when a cloth is pushed over my mouth.

I scream, but the sound doesn't travel far, and a disgusting stench enters my nose. I try to push him away, but my muscles become weaker and weaker.

"Calm down ... it'll only take a few seconds."

No. This can't happen. What does he want with me? What is this? Why is he doing this?

But no matter how hard I try to speak up, I can't even form the words on my lips. Just a faint squeal and his devious laughter as I sink to the floor and slowly fade away.

If only I knew then what horrors I would come to face.

How badly I would be treated by the man who took me.

How I would be left in a cage for months, living on small bits of food and being made to dance until my feet bled.

Maybe if I'd known beforehand ... I would've fought harder for this freedom I love so much.

***

Present

It's been a few days since I saw Chase. I haven't come out of my room. Not because I don't want to, but because I don't want to give him what he wants.

For some strange reason, he's allowed me to stay there, which I didn't expect. He even started feeding me, placing plates of food on the floor along with small juice boxes before closing the door behind him. It's better than nothing at all, I suppose.

However, spending days locked up in a room by

yourself really does a number on you, and after a while, I've had enough. So I step out of my room and close it behind me, listening to the sounds. It's dead quiet. Too quiet.

Has Chase left?

Can I search the home for clues about my whereabouts ... and about him?

Suddenly, a familiar sound ... He's clearing his throat, and something is shifting like pieces of paper ... or a book.

"Morning."

He's right in front of me and to the side. On the couch, most likely.

I stay put even though I'm wearing a very tiny dress that leaves nothing to the imagination. I know he's watching me, thinking about me, wondering what's going on in my mind.

Right now, I only have more questions than answers.

Why me? Why him?

"Why did you rescue me instead of the others?" I ask, not giving a shit about the directness of my question or the consequences.

He shifts in his seat. It takes him a while to answer. "Because you looked ... innocent," he replies.

I swallow away the lump in my throat.

Innocent. Far from it.

But my blindness makes me seem easy. Willing. Weak.

"Because I'm blind?"

"Because you were perfect."

"For what?" I tread closer.

"For me and my ... needs."

I take another step and then another one until I'm right in front of him. "And what are those needs exactly?"

I bend over and place my hands on his knees, giving him a full frontal view of my tits.

I know he's looking. I don't even have to see to know.

Men are always like that.

Since that time in the bathroom, I've realized something. He wants me. I'm sure of it.

I could feel it in the way he touched me, but I didn't want to think about it because it felt so goddamn wrong. But I can use it to my advantage. I can use his needs against him.

So I lean in and whisper, "What do you want from me?"

My hand slides up his knee slowly, inching closer to his dick. For a moment, I wonder how big he might be, but I push the thought from my mind. It doesn't matter as long as he gets what he wants ... and I get what I want.

"You want sex? Is that it?" I murmur, licking my lips right in front of him.

I'm willing to sacrifice my morals if that's what it takes.

Besides, how bad could it be?

It's not the first time I've given my body to someone in exchange for something else. After all, all men want the same thing ... and they'll do anything to get it.

TEN

CHASE

Her whispers are like a drug to me.

I can't stop listening, can't stop fucking zoning out completely as she grabs my leg with those sweet little hands.

Her lips are so close to mine I can almost taste them.

And I want to.

So fucking bad ...

God, I haven't seen or touched her in days, and now she comes out and does this? I'm consumed with the thought of taking her, and for a second, I'm almost tempted to do just that.

Grab her by her waist, tear off her clothes, rip down my zipper, and ram my cock into her dripping wet pussy.

But I know it's all tricks. All the lies my mind spins to make me feel wanted. To make me feel good.

But I'm *not* good.

I'm far from it, and she knows it.

When her fingers graze my dick, I grasp her wrist and stop her from moving any closer.

She's not doing this because she wants me.

She's doing this because she wants *out*.

I'm being used. And I don't like being used.

"Don't," I hiss, pushing her away.

She cocks her head, and her tongue dips out again to lick those sweet little lips that I just want to conquer. "Tell me you don't want this."

I narrow my eyes, unable to pull away even though I should.

Fuck.

It's so goddamn wrong.

She's my prisoner. I shouldn't want her, yet I do, and now she knows.

When I bought her, I never thought I'd succumb to my desires so easily.

Maybe she's found my weak spot. Or maybe I'm really looking for salvation, and she's the only one who can give it to me.

No. I can't allow it.

"No," I reply, lying through my teeth.

But I have to make a stand. Have to stop this from happening before it's too late.

"I don't believe you," she says, inching closer again.

I immediately get off the couch, not giving a shit that my dick is rock hard because of her.

I won't let her find out.

When she touches the collar of my shirt, I grasp both her hands and force them down.

"Don't play games with me," I say. My voice is gruff, saying the words harsher than I want to, but it needs to be said. "You don't want to mess with me."

"I'm not," she says. "I want this."

"Don't. Fucking. Lie."

She doesn't know how much I hate liars.

How hard it makes me.

And how badly it makes me want to kill.

"I know you want me. I've felt it," she says, smirking as though she's found my dirtiest secret.

She doesn't even know the half of it.

I let go of her hand and walk away.

"Where are you going?" she asks.

I don't reply. I can't even fucking say a word right now without feeling the need to scream.

Instead, I storm into the bathroom and shut the door, my fist ramming the wall.

Fuck!

I almost fell for it.

Almost fell for her little game.

Almost allowed myself to commit the biggest sin of all.

I stare at my hands and force myself to put it out of my

mind. But as I pull off my clothes one by one, I can't shake the image of her naked in front of me. Can't stop myself from picturing her writhing underneath me, begging me for my cock, waiting for me to lick her senseless.

Fuck, I want it all.

Raging like a madman, I step under a cold shower and let the water cascade down my body to cool me down.

But no matter how long I stay there, I'm still hard as a rock.

Still aching to touch her ... to claim her.

Still wishing I could make her suck me off without feeling the guilt.

But I won't allow myself to sink to that level. I refuse. I'll just have to figure out another way to ease the craving.

So I grab my dick with both hands and start rubbing, imagining she's doing all the work. I close my eyes and picture her with an open mouth, resting between my legs, licking her lips, whispering her dirty little words.

I want to fuck her pretty little mouth, have her come all over my dick, and make her take it up the ass. I wanna do it all. And I wanna do it dirty.

I wanna do her until she screams my name and begs me for my cum.

And I'll fucking give it to her, every inch, deep inside her, until she's licked up every ... last ... drop.

I groan and come undone, cum jetting out of me against the dark shower wall.

Within seconds, it's over, and the pressure's released,

but the guilt has only intensified.

I swore to myself I wouldn't succumb to my needs, but this was the only way I could avoid just that. And this messy wall is proof of my inability to resist sin.

I grab the hose and rinse it off, then turn off the faucet and step out. I dry myself off and put my clothes back on, pretending like nothing ever happened.

Except, when I turn around again, there she is, in the doorway, waiting right in front of me.

Did I forget to lock the door? I must have.
Is this the first time she came in?
Did she hear me moan?
Fuck.

"I …" she mutters. "I'm sorry. For anything I've ever done to you to make you feel like you need to do this."

I'm at a loss for words.

I shake my head.

Is she really considerate … of me?

I can't believe it.

After what I just did, and what she tried to do … she's apologizing?

Is this a trick to make me feel guilty again?

Or does she think I'm pathetic?

Maybe that's it … because I think it's pathetic too that I had to resort to jerking off to fulfill my needs.

Pathetic. Fucking sad, that's what it is.

I'm supposed to do good and rid this world of evil. Not create it.

Rubbing my forehead, I close my eyes and sigh. "You didn't do anything."

"Then why—"

I place a finger on her lips. "Don't ask me things that can put you in danger."

It's the first time I've admitted that she's still in danger just by being close to me.

Still, I can't help but gravitate toward her. I don't want her to feel this way about me. I don't want her to feel afraid. Don't want her to go back home because it'll never be good for her.

Not that I'm good for her ... but at least this place, my house, will provide her comfort. She has everything she needs here, and I want her to be happy.

But how do I achieve that?

She'll never trust me unless I do something to prove she can.

There's only one thing she wants, which I can't give to her.

And ... her friends.

They're still there. Right now, I can't get them out. It would be too risky. But I did promise I'd send them a note for her, so they'd know she was safe. Maybe I can start there.

"C'mon," I say, pushing her along.

I sit her down on the couch and pull open a few drawers until I've found what I'm looking for. My Polaroid.

I normally only use it for capturing the beggar's gaze,

the one they all give me before they die. I save the pictures in my personal library, and only I know the location.

But I'm going to use this Polaroid for something else now.

"Smile," I say as I stand in front of her.

When she does, I snap the shot.

She jolts from the sound. "What was that?"

"A camera."

After the picture rolls out, I wave it around to let it develop while I search for a pen. When her smile is visible, I ask her, "What do you want me to write on the back?"

"What do you mean?"

"For your friends," I say. "I'm going to send them this."

"What?" Her face suddenly lights up in a way it hasn't before. I've never seen her smile like this, and it's honestly the most beautiful thing I've ever seen. "I can send them a message?"

"Yes."

"But why?" Her eyes tear up.

I sigh and approach her, kneeling to grab her hand, which rests in her lap. "Because I want you to be happy. And if this helps to give you that, even if it's only a small amount, then that's enough for me."

She nods, and her bright smile warms my heart to the point that I almost want to lean in and hug her. But I stop myself before I do and take comfort in the fact that I can at least do this for her.

"So what do you want to say to them?" I ask, licking my

lips, curious as to what she'd choose.

"Hmm …" She rubs her lips together for a few seconds. "Fight. Live. Love. Never give up. You will be free."

I stare at her for a few seconds, but she's not laughing, nor does her expression change.

Is this what she really wants to say?

Or is it more of a mantra to herself?

Regardless, I pen it down anyway. It's what she wants, after all. And if this small act can make a difference in her well-being, then it's worth it.

"There," I mumble to myself as I tuck the photograph and pen into my pocket. "I'll have it sent out today."

"You'd do this for me?" she asks as if she still can't believe I'm really doing this.

"Yes," I say, squeezing her hand a little.

Suddenly, she lunges forward, wrapping her arms around my neck and catching me by surprise.

I'm momentarily stunned, unable to even respond to her outburst.

Is she … hugging me?

Her tits squeeze up against me, and she whispers those same words again with that voice that dulls all my pain and makes me want to do things to her that I really shouldn't.

"Thank you."

It's small, but it's enough to set ablaze a fire inside me that's not easily doused.

When she releases me again, I have trouble letting go. I yearn for the closeness, her touch… someone to hold.

Someone to kiss.

Her.

I've wanted her since the moment I first laid my eyes on her.

I could feel it in my bones, in the air whenever she spoke.

My need for her is strong ... too strong.

And before I know it, I've already pressed my lips to hers.

ELEVEN

Syrena

When his mouth covers mine, I stop breathing completely.

My heart skips a beat.

He's kissing me.

He's actually kissing me.

My brain can't even process this reasonably as my lips start to kiss him back. Feverishly. As if I've seriously lost my mind.

Wait ... what?

I'm actually kissing him back.

My mouth quickly unlatches, and I pause, licking my

lips. I can still taste him.

My body is hot and heavy as he hovers so fucking close to me that I almost start kissing him again.

But that would be insane. Why would I kiss my captor back like that?

Like I actually want it?

I frown and shake my head.

What's wrong with me?

The silence between us is deafening as he moves back just a bit.

"Forget that ever happened."

And suddenly, he's gone.

Just like that.

Too far for me to touch. Too far … to change my mind.

I touch my lips and immediately pull back. They're still buzzing, tingling with heat and desire.

What the hell?

I should hate him. Despise him for keeping me locked up in here, yet … the moment he kissed me, I wanted nothing than for him to kiss me and take me.

It's an unfamiliar feeling to me, and it terrified the living shit out of me.

I've kissed and fucked a few men before … back at Roy's club … but they never gave me *this* …

This uncontrollable desire to put my lips on his.

Fuck. It's wrong.

I was just overjoyed when he mentioned sending the photograph with the text to Ella and Cage, and I couldn't stop myself from hugging him. But then he suddenly kissed me.

And I let him.

Not because I wanted to misuse his trust or to make him fall for me so he'd let me go.

I let him ... because it felt good.

Fuck.

"I'm going to work," he suddenly calls out from the hallway.

Work? Now?

I shift on the couch. "What am I supposed to do?"

"Whatever you want. But don't try to force your way out. I'd hate to have to fix everything, and it won't get you anywhere." His voice isn't threatening, but it's definitely a warning.

"Fine," I say, folding my arms, trying not to sound like an idiot because I'm still stunned by what just happened.

"I'll be back home soon," he says.

Great. Maybe then we can discuss what happened.

Or not. Maybe it's best if we both ignore it.

I mean ... he knew as well as I did what my plan was. He saw through it right away.

But this isn't how it was supposed to go. At all.

***

CHASE

The pen between my fingers furiously sways up and down as I sit back in my chair and pretend to listen to the other board members of my company, Chase Enterprises—a conglomerate selling luxury vehicles and boats to ultra-rich clients.

I didn't just roll into this position. I built this company up from the ground, investing what little money I had when I finished college into a startup. It kept growing, and I kept hiring more people, and here we are today.

We're having a meeting about some schmuck who decided to fuck up the nationally broadcasted commercial without consulting us. Of course, he's gonna get fired, so I don't even see the point in discussing this.

I'm not even interested, to be honest. I don't know the dude, and quite frankly, I don't even care. My mind is still at home, where she is ... and with every passing second, I wonder what she's doing.

If she's thinking about me the way I am about her now.

If she feels the same way about that kiss as I do.

If she can still taste me on her lips.

Because I can taste her.

Every time I swipe my tongue along the rim of my mouth, my cock gets harder.

It's wrong, but my body won't stop responding to the

thought of having her, and that kiss... it pushed me over the edge.

I don't even know why I kissed her. It just happened.

I longed for her so much that I couldn't stop myself anymore. In fact, I'm almost thinking of doing it again.

Fuck.

She's half my age. Twenty, at most. Why am I even thinking about this?

But damn, that kiss was exactly what I needed. Made me think about things I really shouldn't be thinking about, especially not right now, during this meeting.

"Chase?"

Everyone suddenly looks at me, and I stop staring at my pen, stop flicking it entirely as I open my mouth. "Sorry?" I clear my throat.

"Are you for or against?"

"What?"

One of them raises a brow. Of course, I got caught daydreaming. Like it hasn't ever happened to them.

"Fire him, yes or no?"

"Yes."

Another one frowns. "Are you sure? He's been a great asset to this company during the past few years. Two slipups should be allowed, right?"

"Except this slipup got us national attention. And I don't mean in a good way." I put the pen down when I almost break it. "That sexist commercial got the online community up in arms. Our community managers on

Facebook can barely keep up with the backlash in the posts."

They're waiting for me to say more, but I have nothing else to say. There is no coming back from this "slipup." I don't condone these types of commercials for my brands.

I place my fingertips against each other and say, "Fired. End of story."

"All right. Five votes against four. The decision is made," the chairman says, and he nods. "Let's take a break. We could probably all use a cup of coffee, I think."

As everyone gets up and moves toward the door, I stay seated and turn around toward the window, watching the outside world go by. Those people down there … I wonder how many of them are twisted. How many of them are corrupt. How many of them should've been killed.

That was why I had to be very selective of my board members. I don't just allow anyone to join my company and rise in the ranks. I need to know whether they're immune to corruption. To greed. To everything that makes this world evil.

Because I don't want to have to end up killing one of my own board members.

That'd be too sadistic. And bad for the company, might I add.

No, I prefer keeping this place as clean and perfect as can be. Our image must be perfect, so *we* must be perfect. I expect nothing less from everyone in my company. If they fail … they go. Except now, I'm starting to wonder if I'm the one who should be going next.

I've been anything but perfect these past few days. Ever since she came into my life, I've found it increasingly hard to resist sin. I've done something unforgivable to this human being, but I know it was for a good reason.

I had to know if I was just like *them* ... evil.

Turns out, I couldn't do it.

But now I'm stuck with her. And I can't let her go.

Not even if I wanted to.

She's taken over my mind to the point that I'm becoming obsessed. Every damn second of the day, she seems to be all I can think about, and it's annoying the fuck out of me.

What is it about this woman who makes me so weak?

I tap my fingers together and narrow my eyes, trying to think of a solution, but I come up with nothing. There is nothing I can do ... nothing but give in.

Either to her ... or to death.

Because if I ever get caught by the cops for giving those who do evil the justice they deserve, I will take matters into my own hands.

Suddenly, my phone rings, so I take it out of my pocket and answer it.

"Have you freed her yet?" It's Brandon.

"No."

Not this again.

"Why not?"

I don't have to explain it to him, but I'll amuse him. Just

this once. "You know *why*."

"You can't just keep her to keep yourself in check. She's not a pet."

"I told you why I was doing this before we even started," I hiss. "Don't bring this on me now."

"Weren't you the one who always yammered on about *doing the right thing*?"

"This is the right thing. She's alive, isn't she?" I whisper-yell. I don't want my colleagues to hear.

"At what cost?"

"Look, why are you even calling me right now? Just to tell me I'm bad? I already know," I retort.

"Because you're slipping, and you told me to warn you when you did," he says.

I clench the phone in my hand. "Don't …"

"Let her go then."

"I. Can't," I shout back, then I end the call, staring at the phone for a few seconds before chucking it at the wall.

Fuck.

"Fuck!" I hiss, picking it up again.

Luckily, it still works, but the screen is broken.

Why did he have to call me? Why does he always have to remind me of what I've done? Does he enjoy it? Of course, he does. He likes to see me writhe because we're both the same, he and I. We both enjoy witnessing the misery of bad people … and I'm becoming one of them now.

Motherfucker.

Sometimes, I really wish we weren't so much alike.

Brandon can see right through me, which is why I'm so pissed off. I don't like it when someone knows exactly what goes on in my mind. When I'm going down the wrong path.

I know it, yet I also know I'm powerless to stop it.

I started my descent long ago. The moment I decided to contact Graham and set up a meeting. Then everything after that fell into place like dominoes.

The only question now is what will happen?

Her.

That's what's going to happen.

Right now, everything revolves around her.

I turn around and grab my laptop. I turn on the connection to the cameras in my home and sit back until I've found her. She's switching channels on the television, probably listening to the news. I wonder how long it's been since she last heard other people—besides me, Graham, and the people she was stuck with in the compound—talk.

She stares at the television like a child experiencing everything brand new, and it captivates me. After a while, she gets up and starts exploring the house again. It's then that I notice she's wearing nothing but a shirt … *my* shirt, to be exact.

I swallow.

She grabs an apple from the bowl on the kitchen countertop and takes a bite. The juices flow down her mouth, and I lick my lips as I salivate with greed.

Not from hunger for food … but from hunger for her.

Fuck.

I close the laptop and rub my chin, annoyed. I still have work to do, but at this point, I honestly don't give a shit about this meeting anymore. We've discussed everything already, so what point is there in staying? None.

I get up and grab my coat. They can figure shit out without me. I don't care anymore.

I have to do something about this antsy feeling in my body, this twitch that keeps popping up in my lips.

Savage needs are running sky high right now.

I just don't know whether I want to fuck … or kill.

But the decision is easily made when I think about what's waiting for me at home.

TWELVE

Syrena

As I let my fingers brush along the windows, searching for a way to open them, the front door suddenly slams open, catching me by surprise. I almost tumble but manage to capture myself on the windowsill, blowing out a breath.

"Hello?" I mutter.

"It's me." His voice is enough to give me goose bumps.

I can hear him throw his coat on the hanger and set something down. His footsteps come closer. I sit down on the windowsill, hands behind me, pushing my tits forward.

He didn't stay at work for time, which begs the question—why did he leave early?

I'm thinking it's because of me.

"You came home early," I muse, licking my lips as I smile.

"Yes."

No denial. No explanation. Exactly his style.

He doesn't mince words, which is why every single one of them he does utter is important. And I need to pull out as many as I can. One by one. Until he's explained all this.

And I know just the way to go about it.

As he approaches, I cross my legs and seductively lean back on the windowsill, awaiting his command.

He's right in front of me, but I don't move an inch.

His finger touches the collar of the shirt I'm wearing. His shirt. Starting at the top, he slides all the way down between my breasts and to my navel, stopping only when the fabric comes to an end right below my hipsf.

"You're wearing my shirt," he murmurs. I can't tell if he likes it or if he's upset.

I cock my head and run my fingers along the buttons, popping just the top one. "Do you like it?"

He sucks in a breath. "Don't."

"Why?" I ask, leaning in closer. "It's too hot in here, isn't it?"

I know I'm taunting him.

I want him to cross his boundaries. I want him to take what he wants, so he'll give me what I want in return. He can deny his needs all he wants, but I felt it in his kiss … he wants me more than anything.

"I didn't give you permission to go through my things," he hisses.

I narrow my eyes. "I was under the impression I could do whatever the hell I wanted in your home as long as I didn't try to escape."

A soft growl leaves his mouth. "What are you trying to do?"

"Why are you asking?" I slowly let my fingers slide up his chest. "Is it working?"

He grabs my wrists and pushes them back. "Don't play games with me."

"Am I?" I ask.

I'm not afraid of him. If he wanted to kill me, he would've already done it by now. I've faced death. Met him in person. And I still lived.

"Taunting me has consequences," he says, his voice stern.

I open my legs and part them wide, showing him how little I'm wearing. "I think I can take it."

It's quiet for a few seconds. Then he grabs my arm and yanks me toward him. "Don't tempt me."

He clenches me so tightly, I'm unable to free myself from his grip. Still, I don't feel fear. Only the excitement raging through my veins.

"Go to your room," he murmurs.

He's so close now; I could almost lean in and kiss him.

So I do. I inch closer and closer. He doesn't stop me. Not even after my lips have already grazed his.

"Do it," I whisper.

I can feel a wicked grin form on his lips.

The tension is rising. I can feel it in the air like a thick fog blocking all rational thoughts. And I know he can feel it too.

"Go to your room," he commands. "Now." This time, the words have a whole new connotation.

I'm almost tempted to talk back to him. The words "or what" linger on my tongue. But I don't let them out.

Instead, I get up from the windowsill and casually stroll toward the door next to me while I sway my hips. I know he's watching. I don't need to see to know how men like him work.

I enter the room and stand in front of the bed, waiting, listening.

The door creaks and closes behind me. His footsteps come closer.

Goose bumps cover my body as he approaches, knowing that I have no way out. I'm not afraid. I refuse to be. He won't hurt me. I'll let him do whatever he wants …

Everything has a price.

His hand slides across my shoulder, gripping my neck. I hold my breath as he pushes himself up behind me, his body stiff against mine … cock already hard in his pants.

"Do you even know what you're doing?" he murmurs into my ear.

I nod.

I can feel him smile. "I'm a monster … remember? I

don't play nice."

"I'm not asking you to," I reply.

"Good. Because I'm not about to listen," he says, his voice gruff and demanding as he takes my earlobe into his mouth and sucks. Then bites.

Hard enough for it to hurt, but soft enough for it not to break my skin.

"Think you can handle *me*?" he muses. "That you can taunt me like that and get away with it?"

I shake my head, but he pulls my hair harshly, forcing my head back and exposing my neck.

His lips make a trail down toward the base of my neck, where he plants a hot kiss filled with desire ... and something else. A hunger for bad things.

He wraps his free arm around my waist and pulls me close while his tongue dips out to lick my skin.

My legs quake. I feel something between my thighs ... excitement ... something I haven't felt in a very long time.

"I'm not gentle. I'm not nice," he whispers, sinking his teeth into my skin.

I hiss but still don't reply.

"You've pushed me too far now, Syrena," he groans. "I'm going to take what belongs to me now. Inch by inch, your body will be mine."

Suddenly, he releases me and pushes me toward the bed. I stumble into it, then touch my neck to feel a small trickle of blood flowing down.

He actually bit me.

"Surprised?" he muses.

I shake my head again. But I'm still trying to wrap my head around why he would do it.

He steps forward and pushes me down. "Sit."

I do what he asks even though I probably don't have a choice in the matter.

I already made my decision the moment he entered the house. This would happen sooner or later anyway. We both knew it. We were just avoiding it.

His thumb brushes along the mark where he just bit, swiping away the blood … only to dip it straight into his mouth. I can hear him suck.

So he likes it kinky?

"Delicious," he murmurs.

Something metallic slides open. It pokes my skin. A blade?

He slowly slides it down my skin along the same line he kissed me, right around my collarbone. Not deep enough to hurt me … but sharp enough to let me know who's in charge.

Then he pushes it down along the shirt, forcing the buttons to pop. Cutting the fabric in half at various points, he must be destroying the shirt completely.

I'm flabbergasted as he continues to the bottom, slicing it open.

With just the tip of the knife, he slides open the shirt, revealing my naked body.

I don't even care that he can see me.

He already watched when I was under the shower, and my body is a commodity anyway.

With just a nudge, he manages to slip it off my shoulders, leaving me completely bare. Except for the fresh panties I found in the drawer that I'm currently wearing.

He pushes the knife underneath the fabric, barely avoiding my skin, and then cuts through it.

Even my panties don't get a pass.

He rips them off and throws them away.

And I'm left utterly naked. Vulnerable. Weak.

It's what he likes. What he craves.

I've learned that much.

"Take off my shirt," he says, his voice dark and heavy.

I swallow away the lump in my throat and start at the bottom, unbuttoning each one carefully so I don't anger him. As my hand goes up, I pass thick, rippling muscles, and they make my mouth water.

Fuck. I shouldn't at all be liking what I feel. Not at all.

I continue until I get to the top, knowing he's watching my every move. Hell, he's probably checking out my body right this very moment, but I don't even care. It's not as if he hasn't seen me before. This is all a play … a show of power.

He's got me right where he wants me, and he's loving it.

I can tell from the way he holds his breath as my hands push underneath the shirt and slide it off his shoulder. Then I sit back down again.

"Unzip me," he says, still very much towering over me.

I do what he says, unbuttoning his pants and unzipping them until his boxer shorts are exposed ... and the hard dick underneath.

When my hands leave his body, he grasps my wrist and stops me. "Boxers too," he adds roughly.

I swallow again before curling my fingers under the elastic band and pulling them down along with his pants. I have to drag them over a considerable bulge, and it makes me suck in a breath the moment it pops. I don't even have to see it to know it's big.

"Wrap your hand around it," he says.

He's so direct. I'm not sure if I love it or if I hate it.

When my hand touches his dick, it bobs up and down. I slowly go down, all the way to the base ... and oh, boy ... is it huge. Bigger than I thought. Another pulse makes me clench my pussy.

Fuck.

I lick my lips and slowly start rubbing him, wondering if this is what he wants me to do. He doesn't say a word, so I'm guessing this is good. I wrap a second hand around his length too and slide my hands up and down. Pre-cum runs down the tip, and I use it as lube. He groans when I squeeze. The sound sets my body ablaze.

Why does he have this effect on me?

My heart is actually racing as I jerk him off.

This normally never happens. At least not with other men.

But ... he's not just any man.

He's a powerful enigma who constantly invades my mind. Someone who knows how to play me ... and probably my body too.

I just hope I can resist the pull.

When my hands are at the tip, he pulls back and grabs my face with both hands. "Open your mouth."

When I do, he places the head of his dick in my mouth.

His slick, salty pre-cum drips on my tongue as he slides inside.

He fills me completely ... and he doesn't go slow.

Without holding back, he thrusts into my mouth, again and again, until I heave and cough. He only stops for a brief second so I can catch my breath, after which he immediately rams back inside again. His cock bobs up and down against the back of my throat, pushing me to my limits.

"Take it ... take it deep," he growls, pushing even farther.

With his hands cupping my face, I have no choice but to let him.

And for some reason, it calms my mind.

It's ridiculous, yet it does.

For some reason, losing all control over my body feels freeing.

Or maybe that's just the thumping pussy talking right now because fuck ... him fucking my throat has made me horny as hell.

Saliva coats his dick as he pulls out and wipes it on my lips.

"I love how dirty you look for me ..." he groans, shoving back in again. "Love that you let me fuck your throat like this."

I don't reply. I just let him do whatever he wants even though it makes my eyes water.

His hard-on fills my throat completely as it pulses faster and faster, veins thick and throbbing.

"Still think you can taunt me?" he growls.

I shake my head slightly.

He grabs my chin and forces me to tilt my head. "Look at me with those beautiful eyes."

I do what he wants, focusing on the sound of his voice to know where to direct my face.

"I told you I wasn't nice. Still think you want this?" he asks.

I nod.

"Say it then. Say you want my hard cock down your throat," he growls, pulling out immediately.

"I want ... your cock in my throat," I stammer between heaving and coughing.

"Good because you're gonna take it all the way," he says, thrusting back in again. "And you're gonna enjoy every ... fucking ... inch."

My legs clench together as I struggle to breathe. Saliva and pre-cum cover my face, and he keeps swiping it across, keeps making me even filthier. I never expected him to be this demanding. This depraved.

And it's messing with my mind. My body.

Because I'm shaking ... and I'm already wet.

Fuck.

"Take it deep!" he growls, burying himself inside me until it feels like I'm choking on dick.

A loud howl escapes his throat, and then a jet of seed bursts out onto my tongue and against the back of my throat.

"Swallow," he groans. "Swallow it all like a fucking good girl." He holds my face while his hard cock is still deep in my throat, almost making it impossible for me to use my tongue.

"Do it," he groans, and I do.

I swallow it all.

The entire goddamn load.

When he pulls out, I cough, and a mixture of saliva and cum drips from my mouth and onto my lap.

He's probably smirking right now. Watching me with amusement.

But all I can think about is how fucking turned on I am by what just happened ... and how bad that makes me feel.

"Spread your legs for me," he says, and I can hear the enjoyment in his voice. Like he's reveling in the fact of what he just made me do.

Still, I do whatever he asks. It's the only way to worm myself into his mind. To free myself.

At least, that's what I tell myself because right now, I'm not even sure that's the only reason I'm doing this.

His hands touch my knees, nudging them. An electrical

current runs through my body wherever he touches me, prompting me to open wide. My skin feels hypersensitive as he slides his thumbs down my inner thighs until he reaches my pussy.

I suck in a breath.

Hold it.

When he swipes his whole index finger down my slit, I lose it.

A moan escapes my mouth.

He stops.

My face turns red, and I try to hide it by lowering my face, but he immediately grabs my chin and makes me look up at him. "I heard that."

He must be smiling right now. Fucker.

He releases me. "And you're already wet," he adds, sucking on his finger.

It makes me want to growl.

I hate it. I hate it when he knows.

It's as if I've been caught doing something I shouldn't.

Suddenly, he walks away, and I'm left confused as hell. Where is he? He hasn't left the room; the door didn't creak. So what is he doing?

A drawer opens, then closes. When he approaches, a familiar metallic sound alerts all my senses.

Too late do I realize what it is.

Because he's already latched it around my throat.

The collar.

THIRTEEN

CHASE

She immediately jumps off the bed and crawls into a corner. I knew the collar would upset her. I just didn't know how much.

I don't want her to be afraid. I won't hurt her. And I won't use it against her.

I just prefer to have full control. Especially over her and her body.

And there's no way I'm done with her yet.

I go to my knees in front of her while she's distracted, trying to get it loose by tugging at it, but it's no use. I'm the only one who has the key. And the chain attached to her collar is mine to use how I see fit.

And I know exactly how I'm going to use it.

"Don't be scared," I say, placing a hand on her leg.

"Get this thing off me," she hisses.

"No," I reply.

"Why?" she asks, her face still completely runny from all the saliva and cum.

I love how it looks.

I grasp the chain and hold it tight, making sure she can feel it. "Because you allowed me to."

She frowns, clearly confused. "What?"

"You taunted me. Persuaded me to use you for my own pleasure." I tug the chain until her face leans in closer. "This is what you asked for. What you practically begged me to do, flaunting your fuckable little ass."

She shakes her head, but I pull the chain even harder, making her come closer even though she probably hates me right now.

"I told you I wasn't nice. Remember what I said?" I say.

"But you said I shouldn't be afraid. That you weren't going to hurt me," she says.

"Am I"—I grab a strand of her hair and twirl it around—"hurting you?"

It takes her a while to answer. "N-no."

"Good," I muse, caressing her cheek. "This chain isn't for pain. It's for pleasure." When she looks down, I tip her chin up. "For both of us."

I inch closer and plant my lips on hers, making her feel just how much she's tempted me to fall. God, I know it's fucking wrong, but I can't stop myself from wanting her. From taking her.

My kisses are greedy and uncontrollable. All consuming. All empowering.

When I take my lips off hers, she's no longer tense, and she no longer looks frightened.

So I get up, still holding the chain firmly in my hand. When I tug, she crawls across the floor. Fuck. I love the sight of it so much that I let her continue … guiding her all the way back to the bed where I sit down and pat my lap.

"Come," I say.

When she stands up, I admire her body and her tight nipples.

I pull her toward me with my hands around her waist. Then I cover her hard nipple with my mouth … and twist the other with my thumb and index finger. After a while, she can't stop herself from mewling with delight. I love the sound so much that I do the same to the other nipple, alternating until her face has flushed and my cock is hard again.

Fucking her pretty little mouth wasn't enough for me.

I need to have her body too.

All of it.

My hand slides down her belly, drawing a line all the way down to her pussy, which is already soaking wet and waiting for me. I slide my index finger down her slit and push into her opening. Her mouth opens, but no sound comes out. Instead, her cheeks turn red, and her body tightens under my grip.

I increase the pace and start rubbing her clit with my thumb too, making sure she's ready for me. When I take my finger out of her, she lets out an audible gasp, and I quickly grasp her by her waist and pull her toward me.

"Sit," I say.

When she doesn't move, I grab the chain and draw her near me. Finally, she gets it and straddles my lap. Down she goes ... and when my cock enters her body, I groan.

Fuck. Her pussy is so goddamn tight.

Wet.

And all for me.

With the chain still in my hands, I push her down onto my hard cock, again and again. Up and down, thrusting hard. I don't do easy. I don't do gentle. I want her to know that. I want her to realize what she did. And I want her to love it.

Because I do. I fucking live for this.

I tug her collar and pull her toward me. My mouth crashes into hers, taking her hungrily. With my tongue, I nudge and force my way inside, licking the roof of her mouth. I want her taste to linger on my lips. I want her moans to resonate in my ears.

God, I want it all.

As our lips unlatch, I grab the knife from the bed again. She was so close to it that she could've grabbed it ... but she never even realized. Or maybe she didn't even think of using it against me.

But I will.

I slide the tip along her collarbone, and she holds her breath, momentarily stopping her bouncing. I don't go deep ... just enough for a small trickle of blood to flow.

Then I drop the knife on the bed and suck it off her skin. Hard.

I moan out loud from the taste.

"Fuck, I love this." I groan.

"What was that?" she asks.

"The knife," I murmur, licking her skin, working my way up to her ear. "Did it hurt?"

"A little."

My cock pulses inside her.

"Are you scared now?" I whisper into her ear. "Scared of who I am? What I like?"

"No," she murmurs, sucking on her bottom lip.

God-fucking-dammit. Why does she have to be so irresistible?

"Go on then ... ride my dick," I whisper, leaning back with a grin.

She slowly starts to move again. I grab her waist and help her, driving into her with my full force. With my teeth, I tug at her nipples, making them hard ... and making her moan out loud.

"Do you want this?" I ask, shoving my cock into her. "Say it. Make me believe it."

"Fuck me," she mewls, the chain whipping up and down in my lap.

I grasp it and hold it tightly as she bounces on my lap. It makes me feel powerful. In control. I love how it feels in my hand, how she feels on my dick. How we come together in synchronized debauchery.

I don't even fucking care if it's right or wrong.

I just want to fuck her into oblivion. So I do.

With my thumb, I rub her clit while thrusting into her, watching her decline into madness. She's enjoying this, I can tell, and I want her to. I want her to know what it's like to live on the edge.

I want her to give it to me. Everything. I want to see her come.

"Come," I growl, rubbing her swollen clit.

She moans so loudly my dick starts to pulse inside her, and then I feel it … her pussy clenching around me. Fuck. That feels good.

I grab her by the waist and pull her off before I come. With my dick still bobbing, I throw her onto the bed and slap her ass so hard it makes her squeal.

"Hands and knees."

Slowly, she does what I ask, but not fast enough for me, so I pull the chain to pull her neck up as I perch myself behind her.

"There you go … nice and wide for me. Show me how wet your pussy is."

Her hands dive between her legs, and she starts rubbing her clit. I love the sight so much I immediately ram into her with everything I have, incapable of holding back any longer.

"Fuck!" she screams as I thrust into her with full force.

"This is what you wanted, wasn't it? Me fucking your brains out," I growl, gripping the chain tighter to show her who's in control. "You got your wish. Now beg for it. Beg for my cum."

"Give it to me," she moans with delight as I fuck her little hole.

I slap her ass while going hard, loving the pink shade that appears. It almost makes me want to bite her again. But I can't hold it any longer. She's just too good. Too perfect.

And I come again, roaring with lust, jetting my seed deep inside her.

When I'm sated, I pull out of her, and she collapses onto the bed.

For a moment, I stay in the same position, watching her with amazement. Then the realization of what I've done settles in, burning its way through my skin.

This girl was supposed to be my savior. And now she's undoing me in a whole different way.

Fuck.

I crawl up to her and grab her body, pulling her toward me so I can cradle her. Her breathing is heavy, and her eyes are closed. Her body shaking.

She's completely worn out. And it's all my fault.

Rage travels through my veins.

How could I do this?

Why?

Why did I let my lust overtake my conscience? My judgment?

Her mere presence in my home has made me do the unthinkable, and now I'll have to live with that for the rest of my remaining life.

Grinding my teeth, I hold her tight and whisper, "Do you understand now?"

She nods.

"I'm a brute. You shouldn't have tried to seduce me," I say.

"It's what you wanted," she says, her voice hoarse.

"No, it's what my body wanted, but it's not what I want for you."

"What do you want for me?" Her face lifts, almost as if she's trying to look at me.

"I ..." I sigh. I don't even know.

How could I ever tell her what my plan was when I first took her out of that compound?

I can't because it's cruel, and I knew all that going in. I did it because it was the only way to find out who I really was. But I never expected it to turn out the way it did.

And now I have this girl under my wing who is so hell-bent on seeking freedom that she'd sacrifice her body.

She gave herself to me ... just so I'd be more lenient.

Just so I'd be less of a monster.

Too bad monsters can never be anything else but that.

"Why can't you tell me? What's stopping you?" she asks suddenly.

I grab her hand. "Because I want you to be safe."

"Am I?" she asks.

"Yes," I reply, planting a kiss on her hand. "I won't ever try to hurt you again. I promise."

"Then why did you? In that canyon, why did you chase me?"

Her words are like a knife to my heart.

I know what I've done.

I know why she needs answers, but I can't give them to her.

It'd shatter her world.

And as much as it hurts to admit, I don't want her to think of me in that light. I want her to see me as a good person. A human being, just like her. I want her to see me as her rescuer. And I wish I could erase the memories of the canyon from her mind.

"Please don't ever think about that moment again," I ask.

"I can't forget," she says.

"It would be best if you did," I say. "I want us to turn a new page. To start over."

"How? I can't forget what you tried to do. What you still do." She grabs the chain and holds it up to my face, showing me my own depravity.

I push down her hand. "We both know what I like. I won't deny that." I grab her chin. "And you knew, didn't you? And you still chose to seduce me, knowing what it entailed?"

She nods softly.

"This isn't just me," I say. "You wanted this too. Tell me I'm lying. Tell me it's not the truth."

Her lips part, but no sound comes out other than a guttural groan. I know she's struggling. I was too. It's hard to face the reality that you might not be who you think you are. To have your vision of your own self shattered in mere seconds.

Because that's exactly what happened to me in that canyon, the moment I tried to thrust that knife into her.

I couldn't do it.

No matter how hard I tried, I couldn't kill her.

It was an unchangeable moment in time. Something that struck me to my core and moved something inside me. Something I didn't even know I had.

Humanity.

I'm not just a killer.

I'm a killer with a conscience who thought he'd lost all sense of justice.

She ... she was supposed to be the proof of that. The proof of my inability to distinguish right from wrong. If I killed her, I'd prove to myself I was just as evil as the men whose lives I took, and that I deserved nothing less than them.

But she ... she proved me wrong.

And to this day, I still don't know what to do with that truth.

How am I supposed to live now that I know there is a

line I won't cross.

I won't kill an innocent human being. I can't.

But now she's here, still living, inside my home … and I cannot let her go.

No, I refuse to.

Which makes me a sinner.

With her, I've sinned … so fucking badly.

And it felt so fucking good.

Finally, I was able to release all that pent-up rage and desire and take it out on her. But at what cost?

Even though she freely offered herself to me, there is still that line. And I crossed it … multiple times.

"I'm sorry," I say.

"For what?" she asks.

"Everything you have to endure at my hand," I say. I let her go to get up from the bed, gathering my clothes to dress.

I can't bear to turn around and look at her. Not when those eyes are the sole reason I'm unable to say no to myself.

"If you told me why, I could understand it more," she says quickly.

I stare down at the carpet, wondering if I should.

But the more I think about it, the more I've come to realize that I couldn't …

Despite me hammering down on the fact that I am, I don't want her to actually think of me as a villain.

I want her to think of me as someone who can give her something no one else could.

Something much deeper. Something that nothing in this world ever comes close to providing.

Something ... like love.

But can a monster like me truly love?

And could she ever love a monster who's keeping her as a prisoner?

Sighing, I shake my head. "I can't," I say gruffly, and with that, I walk out the door and close it behind me.

FOURTEEN

Syrena

By the time I've stumbled off the bed and opened the door, he's already left the house.

Alone again, this time with a collar and chain bound to my neck.

I can't believe this really happened.

That he actually left. Where is he going now? It can't be work because he just came home from there. Every time something happens between us, he leaves. It's as though the friction makes him want to do something.

But what?

I sigh, but then I realize I'm still naked. I almost forgot.

I open the closet and rummage through it until I find a suitable shirt and pair of sweatpants to wear. They're a bit large, but I can make it work.

The only thing I can't make work is that metal thing around my neck. Did he forget to take it off, or is he making me wear it for his pleasure?

It's all kinds of wrong. I should've known going in that he'd do this.

It should've dawned on me that he had a few kinks. It was obvious from his obsession with knives alone. And now this … the collar.

This man is unlike any other man I've ever met. So much so that I'm still shaking on my feet when I think about the way he touched me … and how good it felt when he made me come.

Fuck.

I shouldn't even be thinking about this, but I am. I thought I knew what I was doing, that I could seduce him into having sex so he'd fall for me and then release me, but nothing is going according to plan.

I actually fucking liked what he did.

And worse, I didn't want him to stop.

The only part I don't like is being left here on my own with this goddamn chain around my neck.

I grab a few tissues from the nightstand and clean myself up. Then I open the door and enter the kitchen, searching through the drawers to find something, anything, to pry open this metal with. It doesn't have to be a knife …

anything sharp will do.

But no matter how many drawers I pull open, or how hard I search under the couches and on top of the cabinets, there's nothing to be found.

It's as if he knew I would do this.

"Fuck!" I scream, smashing my hand on one of the cabinets.

Why does he have to outsmart me so much?

I sit on the couch and mull it over, stewing in my own juice for a while. I don't know why I'm so pissed off. Maybe it's because I'm left to his every whim, or maybe it's because he isn't here to make it better.

But I don't want to think that way. I don't want to feel that way.

I don't want to even be here ... right?

I shouldn't want to because it's his house and not mine. And he is the fucking devil.

At least, that's what I tell myself because my heart certainly isn't getting the right picture.

Every time I think of him, it keeps beating faster, to the point where I just turn on the television to take my mind off him.

The weather lady is talking about what day it is, and it makes me think. How long have I been here? How much time did I spend at the compound? Keeping time was so difficult back then, and now I feel as if I'm doing nothing when I'm supposed to do something.

Ella and Cage are waiting for me. They're rooting for

me, hoping I can find a way to free them. They're still stuck there while I'm here, dreaming the day away, fucking the man who got me out.

How dare I do that to them?

I chuck the remote control at the window. It doesn't shatter.

Goddammit.

There must be *something* I can do to get to them.

Something to get out of this house. Out of this loop. Something ... like opening the door. But how?

The only way I know is with a card, like a credit card or something. I've done it once before, way back when I was still living at the club and tried to sneak up to my room late at night without Roy noticing.

But it only worked because he had an old, shoddy back door.

This house is state of the art. Probably monitored too. Hell, I wouldn't be surprised if he's watching me right this very moment.

Still, that isn't a reason to stop myself from sniffing around.

Maybe if I look hard enough, I'll find a card I can use. Or a key. Who knows.

It's better than sitting around and doing nothing, so I get up and comb through the house again. Too bad he's locked the door to his bedroom, so I can't search there. But what he hadn't thought of was cleaning the insides of the pockets of his old coats.

And one of them contains a thin card…
Perfect.

***

CHASE

My eyes glance over the drawn image of one of the men inside the auction. Now we have a name to go with it.

"You're sure he lives here?" I ask as Brandon drives the car.

"Yep. Checked it twice."

I raise my brow.

"My contacts at the bureau can be trusted," he adds.

"If you say so."

"Hey, you were the one who asked me to expedite this."

"Yes. I needed something to do today."

He gazes my way. "That's the only reason?"

"No. I want to save the boy too. If he's still there …" My hands ball into fists.

"And then what? Keep him in your house too?" he muses.

"No, of course not. We're going to free him."

"Right. Because boys aren't your thing," he taunts.

"Oh, fuck you," I say, sighing.

He laughs. "It's so easy to piss you off."

He drives slowly, too slow, making my temper worse. "Can we go a bit quicker?"

"Why?" He frowns. "Got somewhere else to be?"

The way he looks at me is enough to know what he's thinking.

He's trying to steer this conversation back to the girl again, but I'm not having it.

"No, I'm just excited." I tuck the drawing back into my pocket. "How much farther?"

"A couple of minutes."

"How convenient that one of them lives so close."

"You sure that's convenient? We don't want the cops to track it back to us."

"They won't," I say with a smirk. "I always come prepared." I gaze his way. "What about you? Figured out if you're going to help me or not?"

He shrugs. "That depends."

"On what?" I ask.

Now it's his turn to smile wickedly. "If you let me do my thing." He winks.

I grin and shake my head. "Great. It's settled then."

When we arrive, he parks the car somewhere far from the building, and I immediately jump out to grab the bag of gear from the back seat. I throw it over my shoulder while Brandon puts on his mask and helps me put on mine.

"Ready?" I ask, sliding on my gloves.

He nods as he slips on his gloves. "Let's do this."

With our weapons by our side, we march out of the alley

and into the streets, crossing several blocks before we reach his home. Going in through the main lobby, we find one security guard and a single camera hanging from the top left corner. Child's play.

While I walk up to the guard, Brandon disables the camera with spray paint. The moment the guard raises his voice, I sucker punch him in the face. He falls to the floor, knocked out instantly.

Brandon quickly ropes him to his chair and binds a piece of cloth around his face so he won't scream. Then we close the window blinds and barricade the door with a chair. No one can come in now. No one will interrupt our game.

We move through the corridor quickly, hopping into the elevator and pushing the correct number. The ride up seems eternal, and the dinging sound that plays through the microphones only makes it seem more depraved.

It feels like my blood is curdling. That's how excited I am as we approach his penthouse. The rich motherfucker thinks he's safe up there in his perfect shrine. He has no idea we're coming. No idea what's going to happen to him in just a few seconds.

As we stand in front of the door, Brandon and I throw each other a quick glance before he works to open the door with a small explosive that barely makes any noise.

When I kick open the door, he goes inside first.

Time seems to slow down as the man in front of the television turns around and the popcorn drops from his wide-open mouth. In his bathrobe, he gets up from the couch and screams.

I rush toward him and jab him in the throat, which stops the sounds from coming out.

We don't want to alert the neighbors.

With another punch to the gut, he's buckled over, heaving heavily.

I grasp him by the hair and say calmly, "Where is the boy?"

"Boy? What boy?" he huffs and puffs.

I narrow my eyes as Brandon approaches him from behind with a sturdy rope he took out of the bag. "Tie him down."

"What? No! Get off me!" he says, but his squeaky voice sounds more like an annoying mosquito, making me wanna lash out.

So I take my knife from my pocket and hold it in front of his face. Then I put my finger in front of my lips and whisper, "Shh …"

His eyes widen, and Brandon grabs his hands and ties them behind his back. Then he drags him off the couch and puts him in a chair, positioning it in the middle of the room.

"Now …" I muse, bending over in front of him to show him the knife. "Let's try this again. Are you going to tell me where the boy is?"

He shakes his head, but the sweat glistening on his forehead gives him away.

"Wrong answer," I say, and I kick the chair over, making his head bounce on the carpet. He groans as I tower over him and hold the knife to his throat, pushing deep enough to let out a trickle of blood.

"I know you have him," I say. "How long are you going to deny it?" I grin. "I can play this game all day. I've got time."

He glances at the doorway and then back at the windows, probably looking for a way out. Does he think the guard from downstairs will come? Tough luck.

I nod at Brandon, who immediately barricades the door with a cabinet.

"There, now we have all the time in the world to play ..." I muse, sliding the knife down his throat. "Where should we start?" I ask, pointing it at his heart. "Here?"

He shakes his head. "P-please ..."

"Shh," I whisper, placing a finger on his lips. "No talking unless you're going to tell us where he is."

"I don't know what you're talking about," he hisses.

"Of course, you don't," I say, smiling again. "That's why we're here."

I move down to his feet and spot an opportunity. "Oh ... I know," I say as a devious grin spreads on my lips. "How about here?"

I hold up his toe for him to see, and he begins to squeal. "No, please, don't!"

"Are you attached to your toes? Or do you think you could lose a few for the boy?"

"Please! Have mercy!" he begs.

I cock my head. "Now why would I do that?" I stick my

knife into the sole of his foot.

He screams so loudly that Brandon immediately smacks him in the face to make him stop, knocking him out for a few seconds. Either that or it was the pain.

"Really, Brandon? I'm trying to work here," I say, raising a brow.

"Don't want the rest of the block to call the cops, do ya?" He crosses his arms. "He was screaming like a pig, so I took care of it."

I roll my eyes. Of course, he did, but I like the screaming. I enjoy the sounds my victims make when they know their end is near ... and that they were their own undoing.

Because I don't just go after anyone.

I only go after the guilty.

I slap the guy to wake him up. "Stay with us now."

When he coughs, I know he's back. "Wh-who are you?" he asks, his voice shaky and unsteady. "What do you want from me?"

"You know damn well who we are," I muse, tapping the mask. "Recognize this?"

His eyes narrow and then widen, and his lips begin to quiver. "You ..."

"Yes, it's me," I reply, a wicked delight filling my soul.

I love it when they know why I've come.

"Now you know you can't lie to me," I say, swinging the knife dangerously close to his eyes. "I know you have him, so where are you keeping him?"

He shivers from top to bottom as I draw a line of blood along his thick cheeks.

"We can make this quick or make it last an entire night," I muse, licking my lips. "Your choice."

As I lower the knife and hover above his crotch, he breaks.

"All right, all right! He's in the room, there." He gazes at a door behind him.

"See? That wasn't so hard, was it?" I muse.

But before I get up, I stick the knife into his big toe. Just to hear him squirm.

"Really?" Brandon says. "Was that necessary?"

A devilish grin spreads across my lips. "Fuck, yes."

I try to pry open the door, but Brandon has enough after a while and knocks it down with his feet. "That'll work," I muse.

"Are you in here?" Brandon calls out to the boy. "Speak up."

We look around but don't see anything.

"You'd better not be lying, old man," I say, gazing at the dude still screaming in the chair.

"You can come out," Brandon says, looking around. "We won't hurt you. I promise."

"We came to punish the man who hurt you," I add, and I sink to my knees.

That's when I spot him ... hiding under the bed with a dead stare in his eyes. He looks almost feral.

"C'mon," I say, holding out my hand. "You're safe

now."

But he refuses to come out from underneath.

So I bring my hands behind my head and start untying the mask.

"What are you doing?" Brandon hisses.

"He needs to see we aren't the biggest monsters in here."

When I take off the mask, the look on the boy's face softens. Tears stain his face as he sticks out his neck while I hold out my hand. "I promise we won't hurt you. We came to help you. You're free now."

After a while, he takes my hand and lets me pull him out from underneath.

I smile and ask, "What's your name?"

"Kid," he says.

"Really?" I ask.

"That's what Master called me."

"He is not your master," I say sternly. "Not anymore."

"But who then? Is it you?" he asks.

"No," I say. "You are your own master now."

He frowns. "My own master …" Repeating my words doesn't seem to make him understand.

How far gone are these kids? How badly were they treated that they cling to whatever security they have, even if it destroys them?

My fist balls. "Graham …"

Just uttering his name makes me want to punch a hole in the wall. But I have to compose myself for the boy. Looking at him doesn't make it any better, though, because bruises cover his skin. He's dirty and malnourished ... and I can only guess as to how this man used him.

"Did he hurt you?" I ask, a fire blazing inside me.

The boy nods.

"How many times? Where?"

The boy points at every spot on his body. Literally ... every piece of skin.

Everything goes dark inside me.

I can't look at him.

Not when I'm like this.

"Take him," I say.

Brandon immediately grabs him from my arms and gets up, cradling him. "Back to the car?"

I nod.

"What about you?" he asks as I get up too.

I can't even look him in the eye.

I don't want either of them to see my unending rage.

"Go," I say, putting my mask back on. "Pick me up later."

"But we agreed that I could—"

"Next time."

He frowns.

"I promise. You can do whatever you want with them. Just let me have this one," I say, almost unable to properly form the words without wanting to scream.

"What are you going to do?" he asks as he puts the boy down on the floor and pushes away the barricade.

"Just go!" I yell, and I leave the room we were just in and come face to face with the man who took everything away from this boy.

Brandon picks up the boy and hurries outside without glancing over his shoulder.

Good.

He shouldn't want to watch this.

Even though I know he likes to stick it out till the end. He's always enjoyed the fireworks.

Not this time, however.

This one's mine.

All mine.

FIFTEEN

CHASE

Six years ago

In the middle of the night, a crackling fire lights the skies. Soot and the scent of gas fill the air. With my bag in my hand and my mask firmly on, I approach. On the docks, a car is engulfed in flames, and screams emanate from the warehouse up ahead.

I wonder what's going on.

I came here to kill a man guilty of rape who evaded a conviction. The judge let him go because there was no proof, but this wasn't the only time he did it. There were multiple victims, but none of them were heard. I'm here to set the record straight.

This warehouse belongs to him, and I knew he would be here tonight. Only, I didn't expect someone else to be here too.

Or that there'd be a burning car.

I go inside with caution. I have to find out what's happening in there. Besides, I'm not going anywhere until I've killed this motherfucker.

However, the moment I spot a man sitting on a chair in the middle of the hall, I stop in my tracks. He's bound with ropes and screaming his lungs out. Blood spats litter the floor.

And a man with a knife stands right in front of him.

I frown, watching as I place my bag on the floor.

The man turns around when he hears me. I pause.

"Who are you?" he asks.

"I could ask you the same thing," I reply.

He points the knife at me while the man in the seat continues to scream into the cloth stuffed in his mouth. "Get out!"

"No."

"What do you want?" he yells.

"Well," I say, licking my lips, "for one, you're killing my victim, and two, you're not going about it very smart, now are you?"

He makes a face, the knife still firmly in his hand. I doubt he's going to throw it at me. If he does, there's a fifty-fifty chance I'll avoid it, and then what weapon does he have left? Nothing.

"What?" he mutters.

I point at my face. "No mask?"

He touches his skin, and then his eyes widen. "I told you to get the fuck out. Or do you want me to kill you too?"

A lopsided smile forms on my lips. "It's funny that you think you can, but no worries, I'm not here to stop you."

Confusion mars his face. "Why are you here?"

"Seems we have the same goal," I say.

"Look, I don't know what you think this is, but I'm not going to stop." He holds the knife under the man's throat, who begins to sweat profusely. "This fucker has to die."

"I agree," I say.

The man raises a brow as he gazes at me with a befuddled look on his face. "You agree?"

I bend over and open my bag, showing him the contents. An assortment of weapons for every occasion and for every single one of my whims. I like the surprise element it brings to the game.

"O-kay." He nods, rubbing his lips together. "Interesting."

"Is that all you brought?" I ask, glaring at the knife.

"What else do I need?"

I shrug. "Whatever you like."

He shakes his head, his lips curling up. "Nah ... I prefer snuffing them out slowly."

"Ahhh ..." I mumble. "Like a fire that burns out."

His eyes narrow as if he's searching for clues.

"The burning car, outside," I add. "That was your

work?"

"Why? Is it important?"

"No," I muse. "Just interesting. And a beautiful spectacle."

"You think so?" There's a smug smile on his face. "Thanks."

He toys with the knife, flipping it in his hand, before stabbing his victim in the knee.

The squeal that follows is like music to my ears.

Too bad I wasn't the one delivering the pain.

God, I want to jump in so badly, but this … this is something new and exciting. This man seems to love dishing out the pain just as much as I do, and it strikes my curiosity. I want to know more.

"So do you do this often?" I ask.

"What?" he asks.

"Killing people," I say deadpan.

He takes a breath, his face darkening. "Sometimes," he says, pulling the knife from the man's leg. "Only when they deserve it."

"So you know about the things he did," I say.

"Of course … he's a pig." He slashes the man's cheek, whose pants turn yellow from soiling himself. "He deserves nothing less."

The man turns toward me and growls, "What do you want from him then?"

"The same as you … I want him in the ground," I reply with an unmistakable vicious undertone. "But I like to see my victims in pain before they meet their end."

He nods, licking his lips. "I prefer for them to burn ... and anything that ever belonged to them."

I grin. "Interesting," I say, grabbing a knife from my bag. "What do you say we work together on this one? Would you mind?"

He arches his back and lowers the knife for a second. "Hmm ... As a one-time thing?"

"Perhaps," I say. "Or perhaps, this could be the start of something much more interesting."

A smile slowly creeps onto his face, and he nods while replying, "*Perhaps.*"

"What's your name?" I ask, amused.

"Brandon. Yours?"

I tilt my head back. "Call me Chase."

As I approach the two men, whistling a tune, I can't help but think this might be the start of something new. Something completely different.

Maybe these nights out won't be so lonely anymore.

Even killers need someone to look out for them. And we seemed to be quite the matching pair.

Me with all my toys and passion for blood ... and him with his desire to ignite fires under everything and anything he morally could.

Oh yes ... we were going to be perfect together.

***

Syrena

Present

It literally takes me hours to unlock the door.

I thought the card would work, but he had modern locks.

But I refused to give up.

Instead, I grabbed whatever small metal implement I could find. In this case, I just ripped one of the curtains off and took the metal ring, which I bent out of shape by banging it on the kitchen countertop until it was a long thin strip.

I then poked through the keyhole long enough to make it click.

Honestly, I don't even know how long it took, but the moment it sprung open, my energy zapped back in.

I immediately grab a coat, put it on, and open the door.

Only to bump right into *him*.

Fuck.

Did I take that long?

Or did he come home so quickly?

I stumble backward as he stands rigidly in the hallway, unmoving. My hands are shaking. I don't know if I just got caught or not.

Did I really open the door or did he?

He steps forward, and I take a step back. I have nowhere to go. Nowhere to run. And before I know it, he's got me back where he wants me. The door is closed and locked again. All that work was for nothing. My chance to escape has evaporated into thin air. My heart sinks into my shoes.

"You tried to run?"

I'm not even sure if he's asking a question.

He takes off his coat, and I can feel it brush along my skin while he hangs it on the hanger. Then he pulls open the closet and places something inside, locking it again.

There's a painful tension hanging in the air. Like lightning, it crackles between us.

"Tell me," he says. His voice is calm, collected even.

Unexpected.

So much so, that when my lips part, nothing rolls off my tongue. I'm that flabbergasted.

"I ... I ..." I never stammer like this. "I'm sorry."

Wait, what? Why am I apologizing?

"It's okay." He grabs my shoulders, and I immediately forget what I was thinking or what I even said because he leans in and whispers, "I missed you."

Goose bumps scatter across my skin. Why did my heartbeat jump just now?

I push him away. I can't let him do this. "No."

"No?" He laughs. "It's the truth."

"No. Why aren't you mad?" I ask, balling my fist.

"Because it's only natural to want to run away from me," he says, but the way he says it cuts into me. I don't know why. It just does.

And I stand there, completely frozen as he tips my chin up and says, "I forgive you."

I shake my head, but then his lips crash onto mine, and I'm completely taken away from this world again. He kisses me with such passion, such fiery love that I'm losing myself in the moment, losing myself in *him*. In my captor.

I push him away again. "No, you can't do this."

"Do what? Give you the love you deserve?" he says, and I can feel him smile against my lips again.

It's so hard to resist, but I have to. For the sake of my sanity. For the sake of the people still stuck in that goddamn compound. God knows what Graham is doing to them.

"You can't wrap me around your finger," I say, emboldened by my own spirit.

He chuckles softly. As if it's funny even when it's not. "I don't think it was *me* who wrapped *you* around *my* finger." He grabs my chin again. "And you did it so very well."

I turn my head. "You know exactly why."

"Right." The sound of his voice is harsher. "I'll change the locks on my door to make sure that doesn't happen again."

Well, fuck. I screwed myself there, didn't I?

He walks away and goes into the bathroom, so I traipse behind him, wondering where he's going.

"Following me now?" he asks as a shirt falls to the floor.

"What are you doing?" I ask, as he takes off his shoes and kicks them into the corner.

"Gonna take a shower." His pants follow as I hear the zipper and the fabric dropping.

I imagine he's naked. I don't know why.

Too bad my cheeks already turn red before I can force myself to think of something else.

The shower's turned on, and he steps under it.

"Wanna join me?"

The sudden question almost makes my heart pop out of my chest.

"Wh-what?"

"Figured you'd want to since you're still here."

"N-no." I fold my arms. "Of course not."

"Suit yourself." The water cascades down his body, and I can only imagine what it'd look like. Sometimes, I really wish I could still see.

Fuck. Why do I have these conflicting thoughts? I hate it.

"Where did you go?" I ask, trying to change the topic.

"To see an old ... friend."

"Friend?" I frown. "Why?" He ran away right after we had sex, which means it was important. Or maybe he really wanted to get away from me because I'm finally starting to have an effect on him.

A smile forms on my lips. Good.

"Does it matter?" he asks.

Why the diversions?

I take one step in his direction. "Yes. It does if you want me to trust you, which you keep saying."

It's silent for a while, and I wonder if he's heard what I said or not.

But then his familiar dark voice echoes through the room. "It doesn't concern you."

"That same avoidance again," I say. "Tsk."

"I'm protecting you," he says, turning off the shower.

"From what?" I ask as the draft of a towel wafts by.

Suddenly, he's right in front of me. "Me."

I suck in a breath.

He's so close; I can almost taste the water drops on his skin.

Fuck.

Why am I even affected so much by his presence? I should be scared. Angry. But all I want right now is his hands all over my body. And it's pissing me off.

"Fine," I hiss, turning around before I make an epic mistake.

However, before I can go anywhere, he places a hand on my shoulder and stops me from walking. "I'm doing this for you."

"What?" I ask, without turning around. "Running away after humiliating me like that? Leaving me with this collar? Keeping me a prisoner in your home?"

He places both hands on my shoulders now, standing so close to me that his breath warms my skin.

"Did you really feel humiliated?" His hand brushes my

hair away, exposing my neck ... and the collar. He plants a kiss right on top of my shoulder. The moan that follows sends shivers down my spine. "Or do you just not want to admit you liked it?"

I shake my head. Not because he's wrong, but because I want him to be wrong.

"You're not a prisoner. You're my guest, and I want you to be happy," he whispers, sucking on my earlobe right after. "I like you, Syrena. I like having you around."

"I'm not a pet," I reply, pulling away before he goes too far.

Too far for me to stop him.

"I have wants and needs too," I add.

"What do you want then?" he asks. "Tell me, and I might be able to give it to you."

My mouth opens, but I don't even know what to say.

The first thing that rests on my tongue is freedom ... but I know by asking him that he'll never give it to me, and it'll only piss him off.

So I opt for something safer. The second thing on my list.

"I want to know if my friends are safe. I want to know if Graham is treating them well."

There's a pause before he answers. "I can arrange that."

It feels as if my heart just made a tiny jump in my chest. "Can I talk to them?"

"That ... I don't know."

I sigh. The excitement is short-lived.

He approaches me and places a hand on my cheek, caressing me. I'm flabbergasted for a moment. Surprised by his sudden sweetness. "Is that why you tried to escape? Do you miss them?"

I nod. Tears well up in my eyes just thinking about them. I feel guilty for being here. For eating good food and for sleeping in a warm bed when they aren't. Even if none of us are free, at least my prison isn't cold and harsh.

"You don't have to feel bad. Graham won't hurt them if they're still useful to him."

"Which I was not," I say.

"It's probably why he sold you, yes."

My hands turn into fists. I knew it.

"Why me? Why can't they be safe too?"

"Patience," he says, cupping my face. "Have faith that it will be resolved. One way or another."

What does that mean? He's so cryptic, yet I can't help but think this is somehow important. Like he's trying to tell me something without actually spilling the beans.

"Will you save them?" I ask out of the blue.

I don't know why I think he can.

Maybe it's because he took me from that hellhole and brought me here.

Or maybe I just know deep down only someone just as depraved as Graham could make a stand against him.

"If I can, I will." He wraps one arm around my waist and pulls me closer, his hard-on pressing against my thighs. He's still very much naked under the towel. I haven't forgotten.

"I promise."

I swallow away the lump in my throat. Why do I feel like kissing him?

It's insane. I'm going insane.

"Why ... why do you do all this?" I ask.

"Because you ..." He leans his forehead against mine. "Can save me."

Me? Save him?

"It's why I took you from that barbarian."

"Is that my purpose?" I suck on my bottom lip. If this is what he wants, what he needs before he'll set me free, then maybe I need to focus on that. Give him what he wants.

I lower my head. "Tell me how, and I'll do it."

There's another pause. "As I said, I can't. I need to discover this on my own terms."

He tips my chin up so he can look in my eyes, and even though I can't see him, I can feel him as if he's peering straight into my soul.

"I don't want to scare you. I don't want to be that person anymore ..." His grip on my waist tightens. "If you knew who I really was, you would think I'm a devil. And I don't want you to ever think of me that way again. I want to be a good man."

"Then be a good man," I mumble.

"I'm trying," he says. "Hard."

"Show me then ... show me how hard you're trying." I bite my lip. "And show me what kind of monster you really are."

I want to know him. I want to know what he's hiding. Why he's keeping so much a secret. Why he felt the need to kill me and then love me all the same.

A muffled chuckle leaves his mouth. "You don't know what you're asking."

"I'm not afraid," I say. "You saved me from *him*. Graham. He was a real monster."

My hand instinctively reaches up to his face, and I feel my way around for the second time since I met him. My fingers stroke through his hair, wondering why touching him makes me feel closer to him for some reason. Why it makes me feel like I should get to know him better.

There's something instinctual between us ... like animals that fight for power ... and to fuck.

"You want me?" he asks. "The real me?"

I nod even though he's right. I don't know what I'm asking. Still, I want to find out.

I want to dig deeper. Wade my way inside him until there's no going back.

Until it's only me and him. Until I'm free.

Whatever kind of freedom that may be.

So I let him pick me up and carry me away.

SIXTEEN

Syrena

He lays me down on the couch without letting go, lying down on top of me, pressing his lips to mine. I find it hard to resist his kisses and kiss him back just as eagerly. His tongue dives in to lick the roof of my mouth, driving me crazy with lust.

I don't know why my body reacts to him the way it does. I just know I want him … and that hard dick growing between his legs, poking my thighs.

I mewl when he squeezes my breasts and twists my nipples through the fabric.

My hand instinctively reaches for his butt as if my body

has already decided what it wants before I know for sure.

Because fuck … how could I ever know for sure with a man like him?

He's so obsessive, controlling … scary.

Yet I'm not afraid when his lips plant luscious, passionate kisses all over my lower neck and chest.

I suck in a breath when he rips the fabric away and takes my nipple into his mouth, sucking hard. He has no control over his own lust whatsoever, which is why I'm so desperate for more.

Fuck, I'm like an addict to his greed.

I'm torn between my mind screaming to push him away and my body wanting more of his touch. The noise in my head is getting drowned by rough fingers sliding down my body, lips grazing my skin, heat blazing off.

Just one second is all it takes for me to cry out as his teeth sink into my shoulder. But the pain is immediately dulled by his tongue circling that same spot. His cock twitches against me in response to my sounds, and I know then and there that he really is a monster who loves to inflict pain …

And I'm letting him do it to me.

Willingly.

What is wrong with me?

In a moment of clarity, I push him away and breathe in deeply, wondering what the hell it is that I'm doing. But as the seconds pass, there's nothing I can say. Nothing I want to change. Nothing I'm not ready for.

The only thing holding me back … is guilt.

Guilt that I *should* be feeling.

"Don't think," he murmurs into my ear, his hand sliding between my legs. "Just feel."

When he starts to tease me, I lose my mind as his fingers expertly swirl around my sensitive spots. He knows just how to make me squirm. Everything tingles, and I find myself gasping for air while he plays with me. Toying with me until I moan.

Just like the pet he wants me to be.

And I'm making it easy for him.

I'm being complacent—obedient—and I don't even wanna be anything but exactly that right now. His fingers play me like a violin, pushing my notes until I practically wanna beg him to fuck me.

Fuck.

"Let it go," he murmurs, rubbing my clit.

I don't want to. I'm scared of where this is going. Afraid of what it means when I let him do this. Does it make me just as evil as he is? Or am I just a gullible victim?

"I'll take care of your every need," he says, licking the rim of my mouth. "Everything you want … anything, I'll give it to you."

Without thinking, I blurt it out. "Fuck me!"

I regret it the moment it rolls off my tongue.

He momentarily stops moving, and I'm left with an aching clit, wanting to yell at him to continue. But I don't. I stay put and wait for his reaction.

The electricity between us is almost tangible as he hovers above me.

What I just said changed *everything*.

Not because of the words ...but because of the reason.

He didn't make me say it.

I said it ... willingly.

Of my own free will.

"Are you just saying that because you think I want it?" he asks.

I shake my head slowly.

He rolls a strand of my hair around his finger. "There's no going back if you beg me ..."

Suddenly, he flips me around on the couch and tears off the remaining fabric between us. I squeal as he drags my legs over the front of the couch until my butt rests right at the edge, my face planted into the cushions.

And then he smacks my butt.

"Fuck!" I scream.

"That's the spirit," he says, laughing.

He positions himself behind me and spreads my cheeks, pushing the tip in. My mouth forms an o-shape as he pushes in ... all the way to the base.

"You wanted me to fuck you," he muses, pulling out and thrusting in again. "Now take it like a good girl."

***

CHASE

I fuck her hard and fast, not giving a shit whether it's the correct thing to do. Especially after the way I just came home. But something about this makes me feel good. Something about her makes me want to punish her.

She tried to escape, so I'll make her feel just how badly I need her.

Then maybe she'll reconsider.

I'll fuck the fear right out of her.

I know I'm not supposed to do this, but I'm not going to stop either.

She asked for it.

Begged me to do it.

Who am I to deny her?

So I ram my cock deep inside her, making her feel every ounce of my desire and then some.

I've been horny ever since I finished off that dude. It's what I like, the way my body responds to killing ... and I normally would've taken care of it by jerking off.

But now she's here, in the flesh, offering her body to me like a good girl, and I just can't say no to her. Not when she asks me like that with those sweet lips and those beautiful glossy eyes.

I admit, I'm a sucker for beautiful women, especially when they're as feisty as she is.

Something about her ferocity makes me want to grab her and keep her … hold her close to me. Even though she's innocent, she's far from virtuous. Her mind and body have long been tainted … and I can tell from the flush on her skin and the moans coming from her mouth that she enjoys it just the same.

We're both suckers for excitement. She just doesn't want to admit it. But I will … gladly.

I shove my dick inside her without holding back, without restraint. It's what she wants, so I'll give it to her.

She wants the animal. The beast. The monster.

It's only right that I show it to her … at least with our sex.

So I grasp her hands and hold them behind her back as I fuck her into oblivion.

"How does it feel?" I ask, pounding into her. "Tell me."

"Good."

I smack her ass. "How good?"

"Fucking good!"

A grin spreads across my lips.

She looks so appetizing when she arches her back like that. It's as if she's inviting me in.

So I take the opportunity to grasp the chain attached to her collar and use it as a rein. I pull until she raises her head, and I bury myself deep inside her.

The moan that follows is like music to my ears.

"That's it … Come for me," I growl, smacking her ass again.

She bobs up and down from the sharp pain, but I don't stop fucking her. I won't stop; I refuse to ... not until she comes and realizes this is what she precisely asked for.

I apply more pressure to her hands, wrapping the chain around them so she can't move, can't do anything but let me fuck her. She gasps and struggles, but I persist, thrusting into her with all my fervor.

She mewls loudly as I go balls deep, and my cock starts to pulse. "Come," I say.

And I feel it ... her pussy clenching my dick again and again, muscles contracting around me, sending delicious shockwaves down my length.

I fuck her even harder now, right through her orgasm, driving her wet pussy wild. With a roar, I come deep inside her, jetting my seed into her and filling her to the brim.

Still, I'm not sated. Not even close.

So I pull my still rock-hard cock out of her pussy and spit on it before pushing the tip against her asshole.

"What?" she moans, turning her face toward me as though she's begging me to explain.

But she already knows what's going to happen. She can feel it ... right ... now.

And that o-shape that appears on her mouth again is to die for.

"Fuck!" She braces in the chains, but there's no way out.

"Take it," I say, clenching her ass and pushing in farther. "You asked for this. Now take it deep and moan for me."

When I'm inside her fully, I start to move, thrusting in

and out slowly until she's accustomed to my ample size. She sucks in a breath and buries her face in a pillow, so I pull the chain and force her to look up.

"Don't try to escape. Don't hide. I want to see you. I want you to feel every inch of me inside you," I growl.

"Fuck ... it's so hard."

I grin. "Good."

I wonder if this is the first time she's ever had it in the ass. If I'm the first man to claim her like this. It only makes me more excited.

I thrust faster, applying more spit, tugging the chain when she tries to relax. I don't want her to relax. I want her to feel the real me. The bad me. The man she thinks she can seduce. The man she tried to wind around her finger.

The man who fucks like a beast and kills like a savage.

As I fuck her, I smack her ass again and again until she's no longer clenching and starts to moan instead. "That's it," I say. "Let yourself go."

I know it's hard. I'm not the guy she's supposed to want. I'm the bad guy. Yet I know she can't stop herself from wanting this. From wanting *me*.

Because that's what this is all about ... The push and pull between us. Like magnets, we bounce and attract. And we're helpless to fight it.

I start rubbing her clit again, wanting her to feel just how badly she wants this and just how much she likes it when I fuck her like this. Her back glistens with sweat and heat as I rub her just the right way, making her moan out loud.

God, the sounds she makes could make me come.

But I want to savor it.

Savor the look on her face as she falls apart with my dick inside her.

So I wait and watch the buildup—her shaky legs, her quivering body, the wetness pooling between her legs. And I push two fingers into her pussy, adding to the pressure, making her buck against me.

The explosion feels like the sweet, naughty dream I had a few days ago as her pussy clenches around my finger. When her whole body is quaking, I pull my fingers out and finish the job with my dick, fucking her until another stream of seed fills her up.

Both her holes ... claimed by me.

Like the vicious animal I am.

When I'm sated, I pull out from her ass and let her calm down for a few seconds before untying her. She's shivering and out of breath, so I go to the cabinet and take out the key I left there. Then I sit down on the couch beside her, pull her into my embrace, and take off the collar around her neck. As it falls to the floor, she doesn't immediately touch her neck like before. Only a gasp escapes her mouth, and then she leans into me, resting her head on my chest.

I'm momentarily shaken by her sudden need for affection, but then I hold her close to my body, wrapping my arms around her tight. As her warmth melts with mine, something settles into my heart. A tenderness I've never experienced before. Something that one might call … love.

But how?

How could I love a girl I've hurt so much?

How could I love a girl who could never love me back?

I sigh and listen to her breaths, wishing I could explain everything to her without pushing her away. Without making her hate me even more.

I sigh and whisper, "How do you feel?"

"Warm," she mumbles.

"Good." I rub her back a little and give her a peck on the forehead. "We'll go to the doctor tomorrow."

"Doctor?" She lifts her head.

"To get a pill," I say. "We had sex twice with no protection."

"Oh …" She lowers her head again. "That won't be needed."

"Why do you say that?"

"Graham … he told me, when he took me from the cage, before he sold me to you. I …" She pauses. "I can't get pregnant."

Shock ripples through me.

She can't get pregnant?

Ever?

She sniffs. I tip up her chin with my index finger. A small teardrop rolls down her cheek, and I brush it away with my thumb.

Then I lean in and kiss her. Not because I'm eager for more, but because I want to make her feel better. Because I want her to forget.

"I'm sorry," I murmur as our lips unlatch.

Her lips quiver, and she nods slowly.

"Did he hurt you?" I ask, barely able to stop clenching my teeth together. "Did he do something to your body?"

The mere thought makes my blood boil.

She shakes her head. "He told me when he got me tested. He wouldn't do that because he only kept us there to *make* babies."

I suck in a breath. Rage flows through my veins, and my muscles tense in response. I know she can feel it because she inches away ever so slightly.

"That's why he ditched me," she adds. "Because I was useless to him."

I grab her chin again. "You are *not* useless," I say. "Do you hear me? You're anything but useless. You are worth so, so much." I lean my forehead against hers. "To me."

She sniffs again and rests her head against my chest, and at that moment, I feel nothing but awe for this woman. I never imagined someone like her would be able to melt my heart, but here I am … falling deep.

I hold her close and soothe her, hoping she'll forgive me, hoping she'll believe what I said. I don't ever want her to feel that way again.

"Thank you," she mutters after a while. "For saying that."

"Saying what?"

"That I mean something to you," she says, lifting her

head so I can look at those pristine eyes again. "Even if it was a lie," she adds.

I caress her cheek and push her hair out of the way so I can plant a kiss right there on her neck. Then I whisper into her ear, "It wasn't a lie."

Her breathing stops momentarily. "Then what am I to you?"

"A beautiful gift ... someone who stole my breath and heart."

"But you—"

"I know what I am and what I did," I interrupt. "The question is ... do you?"

"I'm not sure."

"Then figure that out first." I plant another kiss on her shoulder.

"How? If you won't tell me?"

"By accepting my love," I whisper, trailing more kisses along her skin. "By giving your heart and soul to me."

"But—"

"There is nothing out there for you, Syrena," I say, taking her earlobe into my mouth, sucking it, cherishing every inch of her skin. "Nothing but pain. I can give you whatever you need, whatever you want. Love. Attention. A home. Me."

My eyes rise, and I let my hands roam freely across her neck, caressing her. She arches her back and drops her head on the couch, allowing me access.

"I want you to stay," I whisper, tickling her spine.

"Willingly. With me. Not because I bought you, but because you want to. I promise I'll give you anything you desire."

She sighs and turns around in my arms, giving me her back so I can massage her further.

That's when I notice a peculiar mark on her neck where her hairline and skin meet.

A birthmark in the shape of a droplet.

"Freedom?" she mumbles.

But I'm no longer listening.

No longer here.

My mind is scattering, my breath faltering, my heart palpitating.

All I can see is that birthmark.

Because it means … *everything*.

SEVENTEEN

CHASE

I drive as fast as I can, trying not to break any traffic laws. I don't want to break my own moral code, but fucking hell … is it hard.

After discovering that birthmark, I immediately got up from the couch and grabbed my stuff. I left her at home under the shower and told her I needed to run an errand. I know she doesn't believe me, but right now, none of that matters. I'll explain it later … if there's anything to explain.

I have to know for certain first.

What if it's true?

I shake my head. It can't be. It can't fucking be true.

Still, I have to know for sure, a hundred percent.

Which is why I won't stop driving until I reach my destination. Graham's compound, where he does all his dirty business and keeps all the boys and girls locked up tight, doing fuck knows what.

Fuck!

I slam the wheel so hard I almost lose control and crash, but I manage to regain my temper and position on the road before I cause an accident.

Nothing I do can take away this rage.

I should've known something was going on. She was perfect, too perfect ... and now I know why. No wonder my heart is so consumed with her. This has to be it.

Fuck, it's going to be one hell of a long ride all the way down there. But I don't give a damn how long it takes me. Hours. Days. I'll get there. One way or another, he's going to tell me the truth.

If I have to kick the door until I have broken bones just to bust it down, I'll fucking do it. I don't care.

The only thing I brought was a bat and my mask. I didn't have the time or the patience to pack anything else, but it'll do. In and out quickly—as long as I get my answers, I'm good.

Suddenly, my phone buzzes, and I'm growling out loud while I pick it up.

"What?"

"Where are you?" Brandon shouts.

"Why?"

"I rang your doorbell, but no one answered. Did you

leave your girl alone in there?"

"She'll manage," I reply. "I left her some food, and she knows how to behave." I clear my throat. "Did you take care of the boy?"

"Yeah, I took him to the cops. Anonymous. No trail. He hasn't seen my face, don't worry."

"I'm not. I trust you."

"Right. But where the hell are you even off to?" he asks.

I sigh. "Graham."

"What? Why now?" he shouts. "That wasn't the plan, Chase."

"I know!" I shout back. "But I need answers. Now."

"Answers to what? Dude, what aren't you telling me? Did she tell you something?"

I hang up the phone before he can ask more. I'll apologize later.

I can't answer his questions because I don't know if my hunch is true yet. If it is, I'll tell him, but if it isn't, I'm not interested in him shouting at my face that I ruined our only chance to get Graham.

I need to know this, and I know Brandon would never let me go if he knew the real reason. That's just how he is. He wants to protect me, but I don't need protection. I can handle myself. Always have.

I only stopped on the way for a quick drink, a snack, and to fill my gas tank, so after driving for a few hours, I'm finally there. I immediately jump out of my car and grasp the bag lying on the back seat, putting on my mask as I walk. I ram open the compound doors using a metal bat, pulling off the chains with sheer force.

As the doors pour open, I scream, "Graham!"

When I don't hear anything, I step inside and gaze around carefully, making sure to check the hallways. I may be pissed, but I won't let him catch me by surprise. Holding my bat tight, I push open the doors, but no one's here. It looks deserted. Has it always been like this?

I admit, I barely know anything about this guy. Only that he's a bastard, using and selling people as he pleases, all for the money. As clients, we didn't get to see the regular entrance or the insides of his compound. We were limited to two rooms, and that's it.

But I expected him to have hordes of helpers, men who also benefitted from his scheme. Except no one's here. Did he scale down or stop entirely? Or was it all just a ruse and did he make me believe there was more behind this whole operation than his crooked soul?

"Graham?" I shout out again, hearing my own voice echoing off the walls.

Water drips from the pipes, but I don't let it distract me.

That's when I notice the man stepping out from a room ahead. He's cleaning his hands with a towel, throwing it into the room and closing the door behind him.

It's *him*.

***

"How did you get in here?" he asks.

I snort. "That's the first thing you ask?"

"I locked the doors tight," he says, raising a brow.

I narrow my eyes. "Doesn't matter."

He bites the inside of his cheeks as he saunters closer. "No, you're right. What does matter is ... *why* are you here?"

"I'm one of your clients."

"I know," he muses, pointing at his face. "I can tell."

The mask. He recognized it? His memory must be amazing then. Or maybe he taped us while we were there, which wouldn't even surprise me. It's a smart move. But wearing a mask was even smarter, in this case. Still is.

"Are you unhappy with your purchase?" he asks, approaching.

Even though I'm holding it beside my body, I still clutch the bat tighter. "She ... has a birthmark."

He stops in his tracks and licks his lips. "Hmm."

I wonder what he's thinking. If he finally understands what it means. If he'll tell me the truth, or if he'll lie.

"The exact same one," I say.

A pause follows.

The air is thick with volatile electricity.

Slowly, he begins to nod.

The air is sucked out of my lungs.

"The other woman ... was she her mother?"

The nodding doesn't stop, and I'm left with no breath ... and feeling like I have no pulse.

No spark left inside my body except rage.

"You could've just asked me," he says, chuckling a bit.

My blood is boiling. "What did you intend to use her for?"

"Babies. Obviously. What else?" He shrugs as if it's no big deal that he would make her have babies ... and then sell them all. "But she was infertile, so I couldn't use her at all. Shame because I had plenty of potential men in mind to inseminate her."

In a fit, I grasp him by the collar. "Shut up!"

He holds up his hands. "Calm down."

"No. Tell me about the other two you're keeping in here. The others who were next to her in that cage. Are they still here?"

He jerks himself free from my grasp and adjusts his clothes as if I sullied them. But it's not me who tainted him. He was already disgusting to begin with. "They're still in there ... safe and sound with me." His nostrils flare. "But that's none of your business. You're not getting them. They're not for sale."

I clench my bat tighter, and in response, he pulls out a knife from his pocket. "Careful now ..."

He cocks his head. "Don't want to play this game with me?"

I spit on the floor. "You're disgusting."

He shakes his head. "So are you." He chuckles again. "We're two sides of the same coin, you and me."

"I am *nothing* like you!" I scream. "Do you hear me? Nothing! I *kill* people like you."

As I raise the bat, he swiftly swipes at me with the knife, barely scraping the skin around my ear. A small trickle of blood rolls down ... along with the wire holding my mask together.

And it drops ... to the floor.

Fuck.

I scramble to pick it up. Too late. A grimace and then a grin spread on his face like wildfire.

In a desperate attempt to hide, I push the mask to my face, holding it in place while I tread backward. He has cameras everywhere. If they even caught one glimpse of me, I'm done for.

Too late to think about it. Too late to do anything because he's following my every footstep. And he's replaced his knife with a gun he pulled from his pocket.

"Get out," he hisses, stepping closer.

I march backward, clutching the bat closely to my body to protect myself. "I'll destroy you," I say.

He doesn't say a word.

All he does is smile as he shoves me out and slams the doors shut, locking them from the inside with something metallic and large. Even though I try to force back inside, it's no use. It's completely jammed.

"Fuck!" I yell, kicking the door.

Blood still runs down my face as a sharp cut on my ear refuses to stop bleeding. So I quickly turn around and march back to my car. There's no way I can bust back in now. He's expecting me to, so it would probably take me ages to get in.

I ruined it. Now I've got to live with the fact that this monster still lives. And that I was unable to kill him when I had the chance.

"Fuck!" I shout out into the wilderness, opening my car door and jumping inside.

I throw the bat and my mask in the back and quickly start the car. The engine roars as I make a U-turn and back away as fast as I can.

Fuck this place and the devil who lives here.

He'll pay for what he's done. That fucker doesn't deserve to live.

One way or another, he's going to die. Whether it's by my hand or someone else's.

But first ... I'll have to face Syrena.

EIGHTEEN

Syrena

I'm clinging to the window, listening to the bustling people down below when I hear the sound of his car. The engine is unmistakable. I immediately jump up and go to the hallway, but I stop halfway there. I need to put on some decent clothes, so I quickly make my way back into my room and pull out a dress.

My hair is still messy as fuck after my shower, and I haven't properly dried it yet. So I hurry into the bathroom and find the blow dryer, trying to make it look okay-ish.

I don't know how it looks, but I can feel the strands of my hair becoming less frizzy as I brush them down. I pat them down with some gel from his cabinet and spray some of his cologne on my neck. It smells nice.

When someone jiggles the door handle, I go back out to the door again. As the door opens, I put on a big smile and greet him.

"Hi."

I don't know why I'm so happy, but I haven't seen him for a whole day. For all I know, he could've left me here alone for weeks, but I'm glad he didn't.

Too bad there's no answer, though. He just opens the closet and flops down that some bag, immediately locking the door again.

"Where did you go?" I ask, trying to get him to talk to me. "Do anything interesting?"

He leans in and presses a kiss to my cheeks. "You're awfully cheerful ..." He hovers close to my neck and sniffs. "Are you wearing my cologne?" he whispers into my ear.

I nod with a grin. It's surprising he noticed so quickly. Then again, I *wanted* him to notice the effort.

He grabs my shoulder and says, "Don't try to persuade me with little tricks that you're now suddenly falling head over heels for me. It won't work."

He rises again and walks past me, leaving a cold draft behind.

I turn and follow him into the living room. He sits down on the couch and sighs.

"Something wrong?" I ask.

"No, I'm fine." His voice is stern and dull.

"Doesn't sound like it." I sit down beside him and place my hand on his lap, but he immediately swats it away.

"Don't ... please," he says.

I frown. "What happened?" I lean in closer, hoping he'll look at me. "Talk to me ... please."

He just groans and grinds his teeth. "How are you?"

"No, I asked you first," I say.

"Did I hurt you badly on the couch? When I fucked you?" he asks. "Be honest with me."

What the heck is that question? Why now of all the times he could've asked that?

"I don't understand."

"Answer me please," he says sternly.

"No." It's the truth even though I don't want to admit it.

I did enjoy it. Even his harshness when he tugged the chain and used me made me ... hot and bothered. I didn't expect to like it so much going in, and I'm not sure I'd be honest about that if he asked. But hurt me? No.

"Is that why you left so suddenly?" I ask.

He sighs again. "That ... no." He places a hand on my knee and squeezes it before pulling it away again. "I was just ... forget about it."

"No, I want to know," I say, sliding closer.

"I'd rather not." He gets up from the couch and starts tapping on something, probably his phone.

I wonder if he's calling Brandon. Or whoever he met with when he was gone.

It must've been quite the conversation if he's that upset about it. And for a man like him… that means a lot.

"A reservation for two, please. At six. Yes. Chase Marion. Thank you." He walks toward me and grabs my arm. "Let's go."

"Where are we going?" I ask.

"Out."

My lungs expand, but there's no room to suck in the air, no time to even think about what he just said. *Out.*

Out … into the real world?

My lips part, but nothing comes out. I don't even know what to say or what to ask as he drags me along into the hallway.

"Now," he says, grabbing both my shoulders. "This is important, Syrena. Listen closely. Promise me you will *not* try to escape."

I nod.

He squeezes my arms. "Say it!"

"I promise."

"And don't make a ruckus outside. Don't talk to people. Don't signal them. Don't walk away from me, and don't try to run," he adds. "If you do, I'll know where to find you."

A shiver runs up and down my spine.

Something tells me not to take this lightly. He's caught me once before, so he can do it again. And being blind doesn't exactly make it easy to run from a man when you don't know what he looks like.

A part of me wants to say hell no because it's like selling

my soul for a bit of time beyond these walls. But I'd be lying if I said I wasn't excited at the mere prospect of being able to step foot in the outside world again.

And the me that's so desperate for more caves in again.

"I won't, I promise," I say.

"Good." He leans over and gives me a peck me on the forehead. "Let's get you one of my coats."

***

When the car stops, my heart is already racing in my throat. I sat next to him while he drove, and a constant electrical current hummed between us. Like a push and pull, where he's holding on so tightly and I'm almost ready to open the doors and jump out.

But of course, that's only my imagination running wild.

It'd be far too dangerous to jump out of a speeding car.

That, and he's locked the doors firmly. Taking precautions, obviously, because he knows what kind of person I am.

Still, those feelings are becoming more muted by the day. The more time I spend with him, the less angry I feel. Even though the little voices in my head tell me not to trust a man like him, I can't help but lower my guard ever so slightly the longer I'm in his vicinity.

I don't know why or what it is about him that makes me so meek and easy. What makes me so hungry for his approval. His wishes.

It's as if I've finally succumbed to his needs and all that's left is the choice I need to make.

An impossible choice.

Chase steps out, and a few seconds later, he opens my door, grabbing my hand to help me out.

"Where are we?" I ask.

"My favorite restaurant."

"Oh ..." Out of all the things he could've done, this is what he chooses?

"You'll love the food," he says. "Let's go."

He grabs my hand and tries to pull me along, but I say, "Wait. Can I just ...?"

My face lights up when my feet hit the stone path and the fresh breeze brushes against my face. It feels wonderful. So nice that I just stay put and take a sniff.

He chuckles. "What is it?"

"Nothing."

He squeezes my hand. "Tell me."

"I'm just enjoying the outside for a moment."

I can hear him smile. "You know ... you amaze me sometimes."

"Really?" I raise a brow. "How so?"

"The way you adore the simple things in life ... it's endearing." He brings my hand to his face and presses a kiss on top. "Hungry?"

I nod. "Starving."

He laughs again and then guides me inside.

The restaurant is filled to the brim with the voices of

people, all chatting with each other. The sudden influx of noise after being stuck in a cage with three people for so long makes my head feel heavy.

"Are you okay?" Chase immediately asks.

"It's just the number of people," I reply. "It's a bit much."

"I've reserved a spot in the far corner of the restaurant, far away from the other people. Don't worry. Once we're past them, you won't hear them talk. I promise," he whispers into my ear. "C'mon."

He talks to a man who leads us to a table in the back, just like he said. We sit down, and he orders us a bottle of wine, after which he reads me the menu. But all those dishes sound delicious, and it's hard to choose.

There's one that sticks with me, though, but is it really restaurant food? I don't know.

"Is it weird if I say ... mac and cheese?" I ask.

He laughs. "Mac and cheese? Why? There are so many choices. You don't want to try something new?"

"It's sort of my comfort food ... from way back when I still lived at the club. Should I pick something else?"

"No, no, it's fine." He chuckles, placing down the menus. "A mac and cheese it is then."

The waiter comes to take our orders and to bring the wine, which Chase pours into a glass for me. I take a sip and let it sit in my mouth for a while, enjoying the taste before I swallow.

It tastes expensive. Very expensive. And it makes me

wonder what kind of job he has that makes it possible to afford it all.

"So ... um ... what do you do? As a job, I mean," I ask, casually taking a sip.

"My job?" he repeats. "I own a company. Chase Enterprises."

Interesting. "And what's that?"

"We sell luxury cars and other brands that are of interest to our clients."

"So you sell to other rich people, and it made you rich," I say.

He snorts. "If you want to put it that way, then yes."

"Hmm."

"What does hmm mean?" he asks.

"Just that I find it interesting."

"Really?"

"Yeah, because I still can't figure out why that would require you to be there 24/7, even in the middle of the night."

It's quiet for a few seconds. I know I've put him on the spot. It wasn't by accident.

"Certain aspects of my job require me to be ... available at all times."

"Ah-ha," I mumble, averting my eyes. "And you expect me to believe that?"

"Yes, I do," he says sternly.

But I can't help but think about that one time when he came home in the middle of the night and I found him washing something in the bathroom. It wasn't a dream. He was doing something he didn't want me to find out about, and he still doesn't want me to know the truth.

What if his "business" isn't just selling "luxury goods" but also doing something illegal? Something dangerous?

Because it'd definitely make sense, considering how we met.

The food arrives to break the tension, which is unfortunate.

"Thank you," Chase tells the waiter, and then he directs his attention back to me. "Bon appétit."

"Yeah," I reply, picking up my fork so I can have a taste.

The smell enters my nostrils and piques my hunger to the point of making my mouth water.

"Not good?" Chase asks, cutting into his steak. "I thought you wanted mac and cheese."

"That wasn't it," I say, but I shrug it off and put a bit of the mac and cheese on my fork, pushing it into my mouth. I'm not prepared for the explosion on my taste buds. God, it tastes so divine, it actually makes me want to cry.

"Holy shit," I murmur.

Chase chuckles. "That good?"

I nod quickly and take another bite. "It's amazing!"

"I'll tell the waiter to give your compliments to the chef."

"I wish I could eat this every day," I mumble between bites.

"If you want to, I can make it happen," he says.

I stop eating for a second. Is he for real? "You're joking, right?"

"No. Why would I joke about your happiness?"

I can feel my skin turning red from just the heat alone. Dammit.

I should not be feeling this. Not at all. Not when he's constantly doing dubious shit, leaving the house in the middle of the night to go off somewhere without telling me anything. Plus, he keeps diverting every question I have.

But when I eat this comfort food and listen to his luscious voice, all I can think about is how sweet he is to me now … and how dirty he can get when he touches me. It's like I'm falling for him and hating him at the same time, and I still can't choose a side.

Or maybe I don't want to because it makes me feel guilty. Especially if I picked the side where I think he's nice for doing this.

Fuck.

"Why did you bring me here?" I ask after swallowing down the food.

"Because I wanted to see you smile."

God, there he goes again. And fuck me, it actually makes me smile.

"And because I felt like I had something to make up for," he adds.

I frown and lower my fork. Is this what I think it means?

"Because I left you so abruptly," he explains.

"Right ..." I take another bite, trying not to sound salty, even though I am. "Why do you feel guilty?"

It takes him a while to answer. "You know I can't tell you that. Please, just accept it."

I sigh and stir around my dinner a little bit.

"I just want you to feel nice," he says. "I don't want to take your freedom away. I want things to be normal."

I rub my lips together after swallowing down some more mac and cheese.

"And to be fair, it is going better than I expected."

"What do you mean?" I ask.

He clears his throat. "Well, you haven't tried to run away yet."

I chuckle. "That's because I keep my promises."

He blows out an audible breath. "And I will too. You just have to wait."

"Until when?"

"Until I consider us safe."

"We aren't?" I reply.

He sighs again. "You're trying to find out more about me, and that's okay. I understand. You're intrigued, but you know you're also pushing too far. What I want is for you to be happy, and that can't happen if I tell you everything right now. Trust me on that."

"And what if just the truth makes me happy?"

I can hear him smile. "I doubt that, considering who I am."

"But you're just a CEO of a 'luxury cars' company,

right?"

There. I have him.

"Right," he says, taking another bite.

I expected that to be a little bit more gratifying than it actually was. Damn.

"But anyway, the point is, I want to start slowly. Build things up. If this all goes well, we can try it again. Maybe we can do something else next time."

"Like what?"

"Anything you want. What do you like to do?"

"Hmm ... Well, it's been such a long time since I last went to the movies."

"The movies?" he murmurs.

"Yeah. Blind people like to listen too, you know."

"Sure," he says. "If you want to, we can go."

A smile spreads across my lips on the prospect of sitting in those comfy chairs, listening to a story being told. But I can't imagine why he'd want to do that with me ... or for me.

Does he care that much about my well-being and my needs? Is this all just a way to make things up to me? Or is he really falling for me the same way I am slowly falling for him?

Fuck. It's too complicated to think about, so I opt for finishing my mac and cheese instead.

NINETEEN

Syrena

When we're finished with dinner, he asks, "Did you like it?"

I nod. "Yeah. Thank you."

"No problem," he replies. "All finished, or do you want a dessert?"

I hold my hand over my stomach. "No, thanks, I'm exploding right now."

He laughs. "Okay, let's go back home then."

I take a deep breath as I get up, and he takes my hand again. Once I step out of this restaurant, he'll take me back to his home, and I'll be locked away from the world once again. Should I run with the risk I'll never get to see the outside again? Because if I do ... it's bye-bye restaurants and movies. But if I don't—and I let him woo me like this—there's no telling what might happen. Because the sweeter he becomes, the harder I find it to resist him.

But I don't want to be cooped up in his home forever.

Would he let me go if he loves me enough?

Or would it mean I'm no longer able to leave because of my own growing feelings?

I let out a sigh as he guides me out of the restaurant and back into the car. "Are you worried about something?" he suddenly asks.

"No, why?" I lie.

"You have this look on your face," he muses.

"Oh." There's that blush again. Why is he always so good at spotting things? It's as if he knows exactly what I'm thinking. But I don't *want* him to know.

Seems like I have no choice in the matter with his people-reading skills, though.

As we're on our way back home, I lower the window and enjoy the breeze a little, reminding myself that this will not be the last time I ever feel free again.

"You'll see it again soon," he says. "Promise."

I don't respond. I just hang my hands out the window and let the wind blow through my fingers, so I can remember how it feels. So I can last on this very moment, even if only for a little while.

Suddenly, he places a hand on my leg. "You did well,"

he murmurs, squeezing softly. "It makes me happy."

"Thanks, I guess," I reply, licking my lips.

"You don't have to say anything," he says. "I know it's conflicting to do what you think is wrong, but it's best if we just start with trusting each other." His hand moves down my thighs. "If we'd just allow these emotions, there'd be no struggle."

My senses are all over the place as his fingers gently thrum the inside of my leg, reminding me of the effect he has on my body.

"I like this dress you're wearing," he says.

I know he does. That's why he bought it for me. Short and revealing.

He closes the window as I pull my hand back in. Still, the closer he gets to my pussy, the harder it becomes to breathe.

"I like you a lot, Syrena. Stay with me," he murmurs.

When his hand dives between my legs, I suck in a breath and hold. I can't breathe.

He's driving and touching me at the same time, and I can't fucking think of anything but his hands playing with me. Driving me crazy with lust.

"Don't think, just feel," he says. And I do. My mind has already gone blank, completely void of any thoughts but him and the delicious sensations in my pussy.

He's deliberately teasing me, sliding his fingers up and down my slit, and I let him. Even though my panties are still in the way, my clit still buzzes with excitement.

"I like the way you hold your breath whenever I do this," he murmurs.

His fingers circle my clit, fondling me without shame even though we're still in the car and he's driving. He keeps his eyes on the road and his hand on my pussy like he owns both.

Slowly but surely, his fingers find their way into my panties. I feel as though I'm being watched—as if the outside world knows we're doing something we're not supposed to be doing—but I don't want him to stop either.

"Do you like it when I touch you there?" he asks, dipping in and out of my wetness.

"Fuck …" I hiss, barely able to utter a word.

He hums. "That's what I thought. And you know what else?" He pushes a finger inside me, making me gasp. "I can't wait to get back home and claim that pussy as mine."

He starts fingering me right there in the car with no regrets. It's as if he doesn't care that anyone could see us. As if all he wants is to see the heat on my cheeks and hear the moans coming from my mouth.

They're definitely coming out now.

I lean back against the headrest, trying not to succumb to my growing desire to come, but it's so damn hard. He knows exactly how to play me, knows exactly what buttons to push to make me squirm. To make me beg for more.

And he loves it. He loves the power he exerts over my body, how he can make me do whatever he desires.

Like now … when I slowly grasp for his belt buckle and

free him, when I zip him down and take out his cock … he was waiting for it.

I can hear it in the chuckle coming from his mouth as I start to massage him. I can't help it. When he touches me like this, I want to feel him. I want to feel that he wants me because it's the only truth I know to be real.

So I let him finger fuck me while I jerk him off.

The car is jolting, and he's slowing down, trying to adjust to his increasing needs … and lack of concentration on the road. I know it's dangerous, but he initiated this game. It was his idea, so who am I to stop it?

Because that's just it. I was never able to stop him from doing anything.

He is always in control … and I've even grown to like it.

When he touches my clit as he swirls around inside me, I moan out loud, and the sound makes his cock bob up and down in my hands. He enjoys the sounds I make. Loves to see me weak under his palm. It gets him off. I like that about him … it's the only power I have over him.

So I moan louder and louder until his fingers play me so fast I explode all over his hand.

When he takes out his fingers, he immediately licks them off and groans with excitement. "Fuck, you taste so good. I'm going to lick your pussy so hard when we get home," he says.

I'm still rubbing him, spreading his pre-cum all over his dick. But as his hand moves around my neck, I know what he really wants. So I bend over and start giving him head.

Soft, at first, licking my way up and down his shaft so he's wet. When I lower my mouth around his length, he moans out loud too, and the car sways a little.

I grin. I love the way I affect him. That I can do something to him that makes him weak too.

While I'm still buzzing in the afterglow, I suck him off. His hand rests atop my head, guiding me up and down, his other hand still firmly on the wheel. The faster I go, the harder he gets. Veins start to protrude, and the pre-cum is flowing heavily onto my tongue, which I lather all over him. His hand pushes me down, forcing me to take him all the way to the base.

I gag and choke, pulling back to take a breath. But then I'm right back on him as he forces me down. The closer he gets, the more hard-handed he gets, pushing me to my limits, making me cough.

"Fuck, I'm gonna come down your throat," he groans, shoving my face down against his legs. The tip of his cock bangs against the back of my throat. "Swallow," he groans.

I wheeze as he roars. Seed jets onto my tongue and deep down my throat, causing me to choke on his cum. I swallow it down in a desperate attempt to breathe. Still, the cum that lingers tastes delicious even though I don't want it to.

It's already gotten me wet again.

Fuck.

I sit up, and he immediately kisses me. Quick, but hard. He takes my mouth like it's always been his. As if there was never anything other than him and me.

Suddenly, his phone rings, and the kiss abruptly ends, only for him to jerk the wheel.

"Dammit," he growls, pulling over.

I sit back and listen as he tucks his cock back into his pants and picks up his phone.

***

CHASE

I hastily push the button on my phone and hope it's short. I wanna get home and fuck the ever-living shit out of Syrena. I don't have time to deal with other people's bullshit right now. If it's the company, I'll tell them to deal with the problem. I'll be ready for work tomorrow. Not now.

"We've got a problem." It's Brandon.

"What?"

"They're at your house," he says. "Graham's men."

"What?!" I scream. Syrena leans back, and I can almost feel the fear dripping off her. It's not good.

"You didn't watch your own goddamn back while driving home, and now they know where you live …"

"No. It can't be. I made sure I wasn't followed."

"Well, they went to your office first and asked the people at the front desk where you were. They thought it was suspicious, so they called the police. The men left, but I followed them right back to your place."

Then it hits me.

Graham … he must've caught my face on tape the moment the mask dropped off. With a few quick searches, my face pops up underneath my workplace. And my home address isn't hard to find once you have that.

"Fuck," I murmur. "Fuck!" I slap the wheel so hard, Syrena startles in fright. "He couldn't do it himself, so now he sent his goons? Fucking pussy."

"I'm sorry, man, but you can't go home right now. They're inside, right now," Brandon says. "I'm watching them through the windows as we speak. Your ass is lucky I was there."

"Fuck … my shit's at my place."

"Can't go grab it now. And what do you plan to do anyway?"

"You know what," I growl back. "No way they're getting out of this."

"They're out to kill you, Chase. They brought guns, knives, a whole buttload of weapons. This isn't some random search job; they're hunting you down."

I mull it over for a second, grinding my teeth. Then a vicious smile appears on my lips. "Well then … let's give them what they came for."

***

I park the car at the edge of the forest, out of sight, and

turn toward Syrena. "Promise me you won't unlock the doors."

"What's going on?" she asks.

I grab her shoulders. "Promise me."

"You're scaring me," she says.

"Stay. Here," I reiterate. "Tell me you understand."

She nods slowly, but her body begins to shake underneath my hands, so I pull her close and press a kiss to her forehead. "I'll be back soon."

Then I get out and close the door behind me, locking the doors with my remote. I march toward the other end of the small forest, where Brandon parked his car. He immediately takes out a bag from the back, along with a bunch of rifles.

"Bring enough?" I ask.

"I brought *everything*."

I grin. "Good. We're gonna need it for these fuckers."

"You sure this is a good idea?" he asks, placing the bag on the ground.

"What other choice do we have?" I take the binoculars from the bag.

"Well, there's hiding," he says.

"No fucking way. That son of a bitch led them to me. No way am I gonna let him get away with this."

"You sure it's him? It could be an angry buyer. The one who purchased the other girl. I've been keeping tabs on him. He seemed very agitated."

"I'm sure," I reply. "But that's not it. Graham tore off

my mask."

"What?" he shouts. "Why didn't you tell me?"

"I didn't want to make a big deal out of it."

"You know it is," he grumbles. "He's got you on video."

"I know," I say.

"How could you be so careless?"

"It happened. Nothing I can change about it now." I put the binoculars in front of my eyes and peer into the distance. A few cars are coming close to the edge of the forest. "They're here."

"What now?" Brandon asks gruffly.

A devious grin spreads across my lips. "We lead them into the forest … and then we hunt."

We march into the forest and take our positions in the middle, right behind a couple of thick trees. Then we wait.

They quickly appear through the bushes, their footsteps on the crackling dead leaves giving them away. I set up my rifle and take aim. One shot is all it takes to take one of them out cold.

The others immediately scatter while I reload.

"Flanks," I say, as Brandon gets up with a cleaver in his hands and strolls off to search for them.

I keep my rifle aimed at one of the fuckers who didn't manage to escape to a safe spot out of my sight.

Bang.

A bullet ricochets against the bark. He flees behind a tree.

I shoot again when his head peeks out, barely missing.

He doesn't come out until five minutes later, after which I pull the trigger one last time. It hits his knee, and he goes down.

I grab the rifle and take it with me as I march toward him and take out my knife.

"No, no," he says, crouching backward. "I'm sorry—"

I grasp him by the collar and growl, "Who sent you?"

"Graham." He holds up his hands. "Please, don't kill me."

I spit on his face. "You came here to kill us?" When he doesn't respond, I step on his balls. "Answer me!"

"Yes, yes," he squeals. "But he forced us to."

"No, you thought this was an easy payday," I reply, pointing the knife at his throat. "Guess what? You were wrong."

"Please, please, please," he begs. "I'm sorry. I'll go. I won't bother you anymore. I won't tell anyone about you. Please!"

I ignore his pleas. Instead, I jam the knife straight into his heart and watch him cough up the blood.

"Should've thought about that before you tried to hunt the hunter," I muse as I pull out my knife and blood begins to pour out.

When I get up, a noise behind me alerts all my senses. I hold up my rifle, ready to pull the trigger.

But the face I see drags all the oxygen right out of my lungs.

"Chase?"

It's Syrena.

She's standing in the middle of the forest.

Her body covered in blood.

And right behind her is one of Graham's henchmen.

TWENTY

Syrena

I stumble toward the sound of his voice, but the unevenness and countless twigs on the ground make it hard to navigate.

Footsteps approach me, and I call out his name again, "Chase? Is that you?"

"What are you doing here?" he shouts. It's definitely him.

A hand pushes my shoulder, causing me to fall.

"Stay down!" he growls.

I don't know what's going on. I wish I could see. But all I hear is footsteps ... first two ... then four ... rushing through the leaves. Clashing. Metal on metal. Lots of groaning and screaming.

They're fighting. Fighting to kill.

A loud shriek emanates from the man.

Something spatters onto me.

I shiver and bring my hands to my face, smelling the liquid.

Blood.

Shock ripples through me when I hear the cries of the man as his body audibly hits the ground.

"What's happening?" I ask, my voice brittle. Unsteady.

The sound of a knife being pulled from flesh echoes in my ears.

My whole body begins to shake.

"Chase?" I mutter, hoping it's him.

Oh God, please let him survive.

In all the noise and chaos, he is the only constant. The only one who might let me live.

"Syrena." His voice alone calms my rapidly beating heart.

Still, I shudder when he approaches me. What if he intends to kill me next? I don't know what happened, or why this is even happening. All I know is that I was in the car, and the next thing I knew, someone was violently banging on the doors. So I escaped by unlocking it and ran. I ran and ran ... I couldn't stop.

"Why didn't you stay in the car?" he asks.

"They were at the car," I reply. "They smashed the

windows. I don't know who. But I just ran for my life. Toward the only voice I recognized ... Brandon's. But then there was this man. Oh, God." I slap my hand in front of my mouth. "I didn't know he was there, lying on the ground. I stumbled over his body."

I shake my head as the tears run down my cheeks.

Chase's thumb brushing it away makes me lean back. I don't know if I can trust him. Something bad just happened—someone died—and he and Brandon are the only ones left standing. That says something.

"What are you doing?" I ask.

It's the only sensible question I can ask after being taken to this place.

To a forest in the middle of God knows where ... with a bunch of people fighting.

Is this some kind of gang? Is that what this is?

Or is it something way, way worse?

"Stay there," he suddenly says, and he walks away again.

I don't respond. I don't even know what to say to all this. This ... murder game.

What is going on? Why are they doing this?

And is Chase really a man I can trust, or is he the one I should fear?

If he killed that man, there's no telling what he'll do to me.

In the distance, the same gunshots I heard from the car echo through the forest again, and I jolt every time my ears catch them. It's scary. Not because of the sound, but because I can't tell where they're coming from.

Because I don't know who's fighting who … and who the actual bad guys are.

So I huddle away against the nearest tree and cover myself with leaves, praying no one will see me.

More screams and metal clashing against metal follow. I try not to pay attention because it only makes my heart palpitate and my throat clamp up. I don't want to be here. But I have no other choice but to listen to Chase.

If I try to flee now, someone will follow me. I just know it.

And then I die.

I refuse to die.

Another deafening gunshot rings in my ears. I place my hands over them and talk to myself.

"You're safe. Nothing will happen. You're alive. No one's coming for you. Chase will find you."

Chase will find you.

I hear it again and again in my head until there's nothing else.

Nothing but me and my empty void.

Until his voice brings me back from the brink of insanity.

"Syrena." I lower my hands, hoping it's really him. Hoping he'll have mercy.

What if this is it? What if he just needed to kill the men coming for me and then kill me himself? What if, by being here, I just signed my own death certificate?

No, he wouldn't. He likes me, he said so himself. He's been trying to woo me all this time. It wouldn't make sense. Right?

He kneels in front of me, and then everything goes silent. The only things I hear are his rapid breaths and the wind rustling up the leaves.

My hand rises to find his face. I caress him softly even though my hand shakes when I touch the wetness on his skin. The blood.

I swallow away the lump in my throat.

"Are you okay?" he asks.

I nod. I don't feel any pain. I'm just … shocked.

He grabs my hand and pulls me up from the ground, but I'm so unsteady that I collapse in his arms. "Whoa, easy there," he says.

Instead of letting me walk on my own, he picks up me and carries me. I don't know where we're going, but I feel weak from terror. Weak from what I just witnessed even though I still can't fully grasp what just went down.

"Where to now?" Brandon suddenly asks. I didn't even hear him approach. That's how out of sync I am with the world right now.

"Home," Chase says resolutely.

"What about the bodies?"

"Leave them."

"What?" Brandon's voice is sharp. "And then what? Let the cops find them?"

"I don't care. Let them rot," Chase snaps back.

"They could lead back to us."

"Did you use gloves?" he asks, stopping in his tracks.

"Yeah."

"Then we have nothing to worry about."

"What about the tire tracks? Traces of blood?" Brandon adds.

"Blood can't be traced back if we're not in the system. And we don't have cars with tires that rare. Everyone's got this brand. That's why we bought them," Chase says. "We'll each go our separate ways. That good enough?"

Brandon doesn't respond any further, so I'm guessing they agreed with nods or exchanged a gaze. Chase begins to walk again and brings us back to his car, where he sets me down in the passenger's seat and buckles up.

He sits down behind the wheel and starts the engine. Even though I hear the car moving, I don't feel like I'm going anywhere. It's as if I'm simply existing. Still processing the thoughts, sounds, and smells that bombarded me back there.

"I'm sorry," he suddenly says. "I didn't think they'd go to the car and try to get to you."

I nod, but I don't know what to say to that or what he wants me to do. So I just sit here and wait without saying a word the entire way back to his home.

The man sitting next to me feels distant. Like I don't really know him ... even when I am just starting to like him.

But now? I don't know anything anymore. The whole world shifted on its axis the moment we came to the forest we're now leaving behind. For a long time, I'd known he was hiding something … but this? I didn't expect *this*.

This … killing spree.

Another shiver runs up and down my spine.

But the car's already stopped, and within minutes, he's taking me back up to his apartment. Back into that hole where he kept me hidden from the world. Was this the reason? These people who were just murdered?

I struggle to breathe. He shuts the door behind me, and as I stand in the middle of the living room and smell that familiar smell hovering close to me, my throat clamps up.

A hand is placed on my shoulder.

Soft and warm.

The hand of a killer.

"Are you afraid of me now?"

Just those simple words are enough to make sparks scatter all over my skin where he touches me.

I inch away and take a few steps backs, then turn around to face him, unsure of him. Unsure of *me*.

When I hear his feet shuffle closer, I take another step back. "Don't."

"Take my hand," he says.

I shake my head. I don't know where his hand will lead me. I only know it can't be anywhere but straight to hell.

"You're covered in blood," he says. "I just want to get you cleaned up."

"No," I say resolutely. My body grows rigid as he approaches once more.

He breathes heavily. "So you *are* afraid of me," he says. There's a certain tone to his voice that I can't place. It's dark and … melancholic.

After a moment of complete silence, he adds, "Ask me anything."

My lips part, but all I can do is suck in a breath. Is this it? Is this the moment when he'll finally come clean? When I'll finally know the truth?

The longer I think about it, the more I shut down. So many questions … but do I really want to know the answer?

"Think hard … there's no going back once you know," he says, his voice heavy.

My lips quiver as the realization kicks in that we can never go back to the way it used to be. That I can never be that innocent girl from Roy's club anymore, or that victim stuck in a cell … That I'm only his now and no one else's. That there's no changing him or us. And that what I learn might make or break me.

I step back farther as he approaches. I can't let him get close. Can't let him touch me. Because I already know what happens if he does.

But there's a wall in the way, and I can't move any farther.

I swallow away the lump in my throat as I attempt to form my very first question, but I can't get the words off my tongue. Can't let them go because of what it means when we both know the truth.

What it means when he admits that he's a cold-blooded

killer.

I've known it all along, but I chose to deny it. Chose to forget about the night he came home to wash dirty clothes because it was too insane to be true.

But it is.

I knew deep down that it's always been his single truth.

He doesn't just hurt people. Doesn't just make them bleed.

He kills them. Mercilessly.

Chase closes in on me, trapping me between his body and the wall. "What am I?" he says through gritted teeth.

He's so close I can feel his breath on my chin.

"Say it ... out loud."

"A monster." The air is knocked from my lungs as the words pour out. "A killer."

His finger slowly traces a line down my cheek, down the very same path the blood traveled. Whose blood, I don't know. Mine, his, the men he killed. It should shock me, but right now nothing does.

Only him.

"Then you know," he whispers, "I'm not the hero who saved you. I'm the bad guy ... a serial killer."

TWENTY-ONE

CHASE

Hate flows.

It's ebbing out of me like a tsunami, flooding this very room we're standing in.

But I won't let it drown us. Won't let it kill her.

I've gone too far. Too deep.

Even though I tried so hard to deny temptation, she's wormed her way into my heart. And now I have to live with the consequences.

The fear she exudes hurts me beyond my imagination. Beyond anything those men or anyone else could ever do to me.

Like a dagger to the heart, it punctures the very love I

feel for her and reveals it for what it truly is … an abomination.

A love which I cannot have, which I do not earn, which I can't ever crave.

Yet I want her … so badly.

I want her to love me too.

But now that chance is gone forever. Ruined by the fact I lost my temper and went after him … and now I have to face the destruction I caused. Face the sadness that wrecks her… and me when I look at her.

"Do you hate me?" I ask.

When she doesn't reply, I add, "Say something."

She just stays there, completely frozen, clinging to the wall.

"Tell me what you're thinking," I growl. "Good or bad."

"That night … with the bloodied clothes," she murmurs.

"Yes, I killed someone that night."

She sucks in a breath and holds it.

It feels good to finally let it out.

"But you already knew that, didn't you?" I ask, cocking my head.

She nods softly, making me smile and shake my head.

"And still you thought what? That I was redeemable?"

Her face contorts. "I don't know what to think …"

"I'm the bad guy," I hiss, leaning forward even more so I can take in her scent. "Someone who enjoys the scent of blood."

I take a deep sniff, and goose bumps cover her whole body.

"So you're really a serial killer," she says in one breath.

I take a strand of her hair and curl it around my finger. She's so beautiful up close. I can't ever get used to it.

"You're not denying it," she adds, her voice still shaky.

"There's no point in denying the truth," I reply.

The air between us is thick with electricity, and each ounce of truth increases the static.

But the more it pours out, the better it feels. I don't regret admitting it. Not one bit.

We were on this collision course for a long time, and now it's finally done. My truth is finally out there, and I won't stop. Not until she tells me to.

"So you just … murder people for no reason?" Her voice is heavy with emotions.

"Because it feels good," I reply, licking my lips.

"Who do you kill?"

I like how relentless she is in her quest. Even though every word that comes from my mouth makes her that much more desperate. That much more … afraid.

Fear has never been a good thing when it comes to her because it's a drug to me. And I don't want to do this to her, but I have no choice now. She was there; she's witnessed my cruelty firsthand. My bloodthirst is all that's on her mind right now. And I had it coming. It's only fair that I finally answer her questions.

"Anyone who gets in your way?" she adds.

"No one who's innocent," I say, caressing her cheek with my thumb, but she turns her head away from me. I lower my hand in defeat.

"Why?"

"Because I live to punish those who did wrong."

"And you'll stop at nothing? Hurting them isn't enough … you've got to kill them too?"

"I want to erase them off this planet," I answer.

"What did they ever do to you?" she asks.

"Nothing … or maybe everything," I reply. "Doesn't matter." I grind my teeth and look down at the floor, feeling guilty. Not because of what I do, but because of the judgment in her voice. It cuts into me like a knife.

"What made you this way?" she asks, her hands hugging the wall behind her as if she's scared she'll touch me if she doesn't.

"I don't know," I say, sighing. "Blame it on a bad childhood. A mother who left her child with a neglectful parent because she wanted freedom. And a father who overdosed on alcohol after he hit you every fucking day of your life leaves a mark, you know. Invisible. Not on the skin … in here." I grab her hand and place it on my chest. "After I came out of foster care, I took up everything I could to earn my way through life. Studied hard and worked day and night until I could start my own company. Still, nothing was ever enough for me."

"So you turned to killing," she says softly.

"I hated people. Hated what they did to each other. To

the world. So when I started punishing them, it felt so goddamn good. I didn't stop."

She swallows. "You were hurt."

I shake my head, laughing. "You still don't get it, do you?" When she doesn't respond, I add, "My past didn't make me who I am. I am who I am because I love it. Because I love the power. Because it feels … so … damn … good. And I've never felt better than right after a kill."

I grip her chin and make her face me. "Except when you came into my life."

***

Syrena

My mouth opens, but no words come out except for a faint wheeze.

"Is that what you wanted?" he asks, gripping my arms. "How does it feel? The truth? Brutal, right? Tell me I'm a monster. Say it!"

I frown and then slam my lips shut, shaking my head.

Even though he wants me to, I can't.

"Tell me why," he growls.

"Because …"

Because he still saved me from the men in the forest.

Because he *didn't* kill me when he had the chance.

That must mean something ... right?

"You have to hate me now," he says.

"Why?" I ask.

"Because I need to know. So I can ... stop falling in love with you."

Once again, my heart stops beating and my lungs constrict.

I'm completely taken by surprise. And I don't even know what to say.

All I can do is feel. My heart ... slowly losing the wall I'd constructed around it.

"You have to," he says. "For your sake."

He's right. I should hate him. For all the things he did to me. For all the evil he tries to eradicate by committing evil himself. For all the lies and the betrayal.

But I can't ignore my heart either.

"You have to because I'm just as bad as you thought I was. Because I did something unforgivable to you," he says.

Does he mean ... the day he took me away from Graham?

And then it hits me ... the canyon.

He tried to kill *me*.

"You took me to that canyon that day," I say.

He takes a step back, which is when I know it's true.

Everything's finally clicking into place.

The knife to my throat. Him crying. Taking me to his home. Locking me up. Him being so distant. He himself didn't even know what he wanted.

"You tried to kill me," I say. "And then you didn't. But you really did intend to, didn't you?"

He takes another step back while I brace myself against the wall.

"Yes."

The answer is finite.

No denial. No deviations.

This is the one single truth.

I should've realized it all along.

He never wanted me alive.

"Why?" Tears well up in my eyes.

"Because I knew I was just as evil as the people I killed. I needed to know if I could do what they did … if I could even take an innocent life …"

"So you chose me?" I say through gritted teeth.

"You were as innocent as can be," he says.

My blood is boiling right now. "I was an experiment?"

"To a certain extent … yes."

I move across the room and grab the nearest sharp thing I can find. A letter opener. He left it on the cabinet. It's not a knife, but it'll do. I need something to protect myself … from him.

If he wanted to kill me once, he could try again.

"I won't hurt you," he says.

"How can I trust anything you say?" I reply, tears streaming down my face. "You just told me to my face that I was supposed to *die* that day!"

Just uttering the words make them so much more painful.

"Tell me it isn't true," I hiss.

"Yes," he says. "It's true."

My heart shatters into a million pieces.

I knew he attempted it in the canyon … but I never thought he truly meant it. I just thought he was scared, or maybe that I'd done something to anger him.

But none of that was true.

I was just a test to him.

A test to see if he could do it.

If he could become a true monster.

When he tries to approach, I hold up the letter opener like a weapon and say, "Stay back."

"I did what I did because I needed to know the truth. I expected you to die, yes," he says, "but you didn't."

"That doesn't change a thing!"

"Yes, it does. Because it made me realize that I wasn't completely evil. That I still have morals. That I still have something to live for. *You.*"

"No," I snap, my hands shaking with rage. "You don't get to say that. Don't you try to mess with me."

"I'm not," he says. "It's the truth. When I had you, captured you … I couldn't kill you. No matter how hard I tried. I couldn't because of your tears. Because of your face. Because of how badly I wanted to be human for you. You … broke me, Syrena."

"Shut up," I hiss, wishing I could turn off my hearing.

I don't want to hear the words that'll only unravel me more.

"I took you home because that was all I knew I could do," he says. "Because I knew I'd fucked up. I never expected it to happen the way it did. And that I'd have you … and didn't have a clue what to do with you. But the more time I spent with you, the more lost I felt."

"Don't," I hiss. "Don't you turn me into the bad guy."

"I never said you were," he says. "*I am*. I'm the bad guy for putting my own needs first." He sinks to his knees. I can hear them hit the floor. "So all this time, while you've been here … I've been thinking of ways to make things right. To give you everything you need and more. To make your heart happy again. Because I took your innocence away from you, and I can never give that back."

His voice is faltering, just like mine was. Just like my hands are right now as I try to hold the letter opener steady as I come closer toward him.

"Do it," he says. "Kill me."

My body freezes. "What?"

"Kill me like I tried to kill you. Give me what I deserve. Inflict all the pain you want to on me."

"Why would you say that?" I shout, tasting the salt of my own tears. "Why now?"

"Because I deserve it. Because it makes you happy," he says. "I have my arms behind my back. I won't hurt you. I won't fight. I'll let you do whatever you want."

"No," I hiss. "You can't do this."

"Why? This is what you've wanted for so long, right? To end your own suffering?"

How can he say that like it doesn't mean anything to him? As if his own life doesn't matter?

"You're not supposed to just surrender and make it easy!"

"But it's what you want ... what you need. And I want to make you happy."

Happy? I don't even know what that is anymore.

"How can I be happy if you turn me into a murderer too?" I yell.

He doesn't reply.

And the longer this silence hangs between us, the more the hatred flows out of me ... and the more it leaves sadness behind.

The letter opener drops from my hand.

"How could you do this?" I mutter.

"I just want what's best for you."

"But you used me. Used me like some kind of experiment, and when you didn't get the outcome you thought you would, you just kept it going."

"And I'll accept all responsibility for that."

"No." I shake my head. "You can't take the easy way out." I mull over these last few words because they're so damn hard to say. But I want them out there. I want them to be real. So I force myself to say it.

"You'll have the rest of your life to make it up."

I can hear him move from the floor. "What?"

"You want to stop being evil? Then do the right thing. For once."

I can hear him shuffle closer, and I don't stop him. Not even when he wraps his arms around me and pulls me into his embrace.

And I cry. I cry harder than I ever have before.

Because this man … this murderer … this monster …

Is the only man I couldn't ever kill.

TWENTY-TWO

CHASE

I can't stop myself from holding her close. Don't want to let go. Don't want to stop smelling her delicious scents as I bury my nose in her hair.

This one girl has become my undoing … and I regret nothing.

My secrets are finally out in the open, and it feels freeing.

Empowering.

Because the worst has happened … and we're both still here.

Even though she tried to hurt me, she couldn't.

Her dropping that letter opener was all the proof I

needed. She needs me just as much as I need her. Even though she probably hates herself for it, despises me for it, she can't deny the power that I hold over her heart.

"I'll take care of you," I whisper. "I promise."

"But you're ... a killer," she replies.

I grab her chin and lift her head up. "But I'll never, ever hurt you again. Do you believe me?"

She nods softly, but her pristine eyes are still filled with tears. She's so pretty even when she cries. And I'm just ... me, a vicious brute who revels in other people's suffering.

But not hers.

Her pain ruins me. Makes me want to lash out. Makes me want to protect her, love her, kiss her.

So I do. I press my lips to hers, claiming her mouth, despite knowing full well that she hates me right now. I don't care what the consequences are. I just want to give myself to her fully—without all the lies, without all the betrayal.

With her still in my arms, I back away into the bathroom, never taking my lips off her. She tastes too good, too sinful to stop. Even though we're covered in blood and sweat, and our bodies are shaking from all the adrenaline pumping through our veins, I still can't stop myself from wanting every single inch of her body.

Her mouth consumes me.

Twists my heart into a contorted mess until it contains nothing but love and devotion.

My kisses are frantic, hyper sexual, driven by the need to

drown out the pain inside her mind.

And after a while, she even starts to kiss me back.

My fingers undo the zipper on her dress and pull it down, ripping it off her shoulders until it drops to the floor. I tear away her panties and lift her up, smacking us both against the wall as I kiss her senseless. Her naked body quivers against mine, goose bumps scattering as my mouth locks with hers.

Her legs wrap around my waist as I squeeze her ass and groan into her mouth. My tongue circles around hers, and I lick the roof of her mouth. But no matter how many times I kiss her, it's never enough. I always want more of this beautiful creature I call mine.

When our lips momentarily unlatch to take a breath, I whisper, "Still afraid of me?"

Her swollen pink lips show a hint of a smile as she bites her bottom lip. "I …"

"You don't have to answer," I murmur, pressing sweet kisses onto her neck. "I already know the truth."

She *wants* to fear me. *Needs* to hate me. But neither of those things are truly possible if you're in love with someone. Even if she despises her own heart for falling so easily, it was inevitable.

My tongue leaves lavish licks on her neck and tits, and I take her nipple into my mouth and suck until it's hard, then do the same to the other one, twisting them around my tongue until she moans.

"Tell me to stop," I whisper, pressing my hard-on

against her. "Tell me that I'm a monster and that you hate me."

"I hate you," she whispers through her moans. "Don't stop."

I grin as I twist her nipple until she squeals. "You're going to regret that."

With her ass still in the palms of my hands, I lift her up and bring her into the shower, turning it on. I don't give a shit that I'm still dressed and that everything will get wet. I want her here—wet, wild, right now.

I place her down and take off the shirt sticking to my body. The water pours down on her face and washes away the blood. With a raging boner, I stay put, waiting for her to make a move, waiting for her to decide what to do. I lift my head and let the water cascade down on me, washing away my sins and every shred of evidence.

But none of it will ever get erased from her mind.

"I don't want to force myself on you," I say, licking the droplets of water off my lips, wishing I could lick hers instead.

"You aren't," she replies. "I'm letting you do this."

Her hands touch my chest and alert all my senses. I look down at her, shocked at her fearlessness. Admiring her tenacity and ferocity.

Her hand slowly slides down my body, undoing the button of my pants, slowly forcing it down over my cock which bobs up and down when freed. I feel huge as I tower over her, but even as her hands wrap neatly around my dick, she's not pulling back.

I groan as she moves her fingers right around the tip and back again, making me want to thrust. It's so damn hard to hold back, but this is important. She needs to be the one to decide.

But she doesn't stop. Doesn't hold back.

Keeps going until pre-cum drips out of my cock, until veins protrude the skin, until my balls tighten from her fondling me.

God, I want to fucking come so hard right now. I want to cover her with my cum and then some. I want to lick her, collar her, bite her, suck up the blood, and do it all over again.

I'm a sick bastard without remorse.

And despite knowing all that, she still wants me.

Both her hands wrap around my length and jerk me off until I'm about to burst. But then she goes to her knees and takes me into her mouth, sucking me off.

Fuck, it feels so good.

Her tongue circling around, saliva making it wet and hard, and I just want to thrust inside.

So I do. Each time a little more until she lets go completely and allows me to fuck her face.

Just like before, only this time it was her idea. Her needs above mine.

And I want to give it to her. Give her whatever she desires.

So I ask, "Is this what you want?"

She nods, moaning when I bury myself inside her.

Her eyes open wide even though she can't see, but she knows how much I like to peer into her sparkling white eyes.

I can't stop myself from grabbing her face and fucking her even harder. Hard enough to make the tears pop into her eyes and gargling sounds emerge from her throat.

But despite shoving my dick even farther down her throat, she doesn't push me away. Instead, she parts her legs and begins to touch herself, flicking her clit until she trembles from lust.

"You don't have to do this," I say as I pull out to let her breathe.

But she refuses to say anything to deny me this.

"Tell me you don't want this," I say, lifting her chin.

She shakes her head. "I do."

I frown. "Why?"

"Do you know why you feel the need to kill?"

"No," I answer. "I just do."

She licks her lips. "Then you understand why I don't know the reason I need to feel you inside me."

I nod. I finally understand. We both have our wicked needs. She just found her own when she met me. Maybe that's why she's struggled so much, hated me so much ... because I brought out the worst in her.

But now she's finally learning to accept that. Even though it shouldn't, it makes perfect sense.

She ... is perfect.

And when she opens her mouth, I don't hold back. I shove right back in and hold her lips right where I want them to be, against my skin, with my tip bobbing against the back of her throat. She coughs and heaves when I pull back out, but her mouth is still wide open for me to claim, so I do. I thrust back inside with full force, taking all my pent-up adrenaline and rage from back in the forest out on her.

I know it's wrong. But she likes it wrong. And she's about to come.

Her whole body is shaking, sweating, her face turning red.

She's so close, and she knows exactly where to touch herself to push herself over the edge.

So I bury myself deep inside her and growl, "Come."

Her moans fill me with hunger, and as she comes, so do I.

My seed jets out onto her tongue, and she swallows it all down. I don't even have to tell her ... she's that greedy for more.

When I pull out, I'm still hard, still turned on. I grab her arms and pull her up from the ground, smashing my lips on hers. I need to taste her and have every inch of her.

My hand instinctively finds its way to her sweet spot, sliding my fingers down her slit until she mewls in my mouth. Her nub is still swollen, still responding to my touch. I'm not the only one hungry for more.

I lift her up again, her legs clinging to my back as I push her against the wall and lower her onto my dick. We fuck, hard and fast, like animals in heat. Not even when I turn down the warmth of the shower can the water cool us down.

I cover her mouth with mine, sucking up her moans as I thrust deep inside her. I want to take from her until nothing's left but a panting mess. And when our mouths unlatch, I can't help myself from sinking my teeth into her shoulder until she cries out a mixture of pain and relief.

And I suck up the blood and lick her skin until she's moaning again, and all the bunched-up frustration comes pouring out. We meld together in one feverish pool of lust, clinging to each other, desperately trying to get closer.

Her breathing is ragged, and her skin is red as I whisper into her ear, "Come for me. I want to feel you."

Her pussy contracts around me, and she moans out loud from the orgasm.

Her muscles are milking me to the point where my balls tighten, and I explode. Roaring out loud, I come deep inside her, filling her up to the brim.

When we're both finally sated, I let her down again and hug her tight as we finish our shower together. When we're both dry, I take her to my room and lay down with her on the bed, wrapping my arm tightly around her.

"Hmm …"

"What is it?" I ask, taking in the scent of her hair.

"You've never brought me to your room before," she says, smiling.

"I take it you like my bed then?"

"It's very soft ... and comfy ... and warm," she murmurs, turning around in my arms so she can snuggle into my chest. "I like it when you stop putting up barriers."

"Hmm ..." Now it's my turn not to know what to say.

I admit, I have been putting up wall after wall just to keep her from getting more upset. But part of that was because of my own selfishness. My own inability to truly let her experience freedom is what makes her life so hard right now. And I feel guilty for putting all that on her. For making her stay.

Does she even want to? Especially after knowing what kind of a monster I really am?

"Can I ask you something?" she suddenly murmurs.

"Anything."

"Who were those men in the woods? The ones you killed?"

I swallow and take a deep breath. "Graham's men."

She places a hand on my chest. "What were they doing there?"

"I went to Graham. I intended to kill him but failed."

"So they came after you," she says in a single breath.

I nod. "And most likely you too. Probably wanted you back in his claws." My blood already begins to boil from the mere thought of him putting her back in the cage.

"But I'm with you now. I'm safe," she mumbles, burying her face against me.

A glow spreads throughout my body, instantly replacing the building rage. I don't know why she makes me feel the way I do, but I honestly want nothing more than to protect her.

"Thank you," she says after a while.

"For what?"

I haven't done anything good.

"For telling the truth," she says.

"Oh."

"And for trying to kill Graham," she adds. "Did you go there because of me?"

I lick my lips and smile. "Yes. I wanted him to suffer for the pain he caused." But I also wanted to know the facts. Something I can't tell her because it'll definitely kill her.

And as she turns around in my arms and curls back, I can't help but stare at the walls ahead, wondering when … *if* I'm ever going to be courageous enough to tell her why I had to talk to him.

I don't want to lose her.

But I fear I definitely will.

TWENTY-THREE

CHASE

A few weeks later

I wake up to the sound of my phone buzzing. At first, it doesn't even register. All I can do is smile and take a whiff of Syrena's scent again, relishing in the fact that she's mine ... that she's still here ... and that she isn't afraid, despite all the things she experienced.

We've been growing closer over the past few weeks, and it's surprising to this day that she's accepted all my darkness so easily. When I asked her if she still wanted me, she didn't lie. When I asked her if she hated that I was a killer, she didn't say yes. And when I told her I couldn't stop doing what I do best ... she didn't deny me my needs.

She's so strong. I admire her. And I feel so goddamn lucky to wake up next to her … and that she hasn't run away. She's so goddamn perfect, it almost hurts.

With hazy eyes and a rumbling stomach, I pick my phone up from the cabinet and stare at the number on the screen. Brandon? What does he want?

"Yeah?" I say, picking it up as I get out of bed to yawn.

"Did you see the news? They found the bodies."

"Hold on, I have to put on something first," I grumble, stepping out of the room so I don't wake her.

"Okay," he replies as I put on some shorts.

"Yeah, I've seen it. And?" I say, thinking about the moment I saw it on the news and immediately turned it off. I've been keeping Syrena away from the television ever since the news broke out. I don't want her to relive that stuff. "Anything special?"

"Police aren't saying much, but I talked to my guy on the inside, and he says they don't have a clue who could've done it. They just think it's a feud between mafia families or some shit."

"Fine with me."

"So you're not worried at all?"

"They won't find us. They never do," I reply.

"Right. Well, I've got other news too that I thought you might want to know …"

"What is it? Cut the suspense," I growl.

"Graham's gone."

My eyes widen, and I clasp the phone tighter. "What?

How? When?"

"I don't know. I just got the news from one of my other contacts at the police. They think he's dead."

"You're sure about this?"

"It's looking like it. There's blood everywhere in the compound, and all the cages were empty too."

"What about the others that were there?" I ask. "A woman and a man."

"The girl's been found. The guy's missing."

I slam my fist on the table but then remember to be quiet. "Fuck," I hiss. "I wanted to go kill him myself."

"Should've done it when you had the chance."

"I know, all right!" I bark. "Just tell me if we can find the two. I want to make sure they're safe at the very least."

"Okay, well what do you want me to do?"

"Fuck, I don't know. We have to do whatever we can to find them. I promised Syrena. And we have to make sure Graham's dead."

"I'll ask my connections. Hopefully, we can pinpoint their location. The girl shouldn't be too hard, but I don't know about the other one."

"Right. Also, find out what the fuck happened to Graham. I don't care how much time it takes or how hard it is to find the information. Just get it. I want that son of a bitch down under the ground before he even attempts to contact me. I don't want Syrena finding out about him or their connection. Ever."

"Their connection? What are you talking about?"

Of course, I hadn't told him yet. I just forgot. "He had her mother too." I hiss. "And that ain't even half of it ..."

"Holy shit."

"Yes. So do your fucking best to get a hold of them. *All* of them."

"Got it," Brandon replies.

"Thanks," I say.

"No problem," he says, before I hang up the phone.

I close my eyes and take a deep breath, trying to put things away in my mind.

That's when I hear her voice behind me. "Who was that?"

"Oh ... just Brandon," I say, smiling as I turn around.

"You were talking about Graham," she says.

"Yeah. It's nothing important."

"It is," she says.

Her tenacious voice makes me swallow away the lump in my throat.

"You said something about him having my mother too?"

My face contorts, and my lungs constrict.

Fuck.

Fuck. Fuck. Fuck!

How much did she hear?

Too much.

It's too late to deny things now. She knows what she heard, and I doubt I can ever spin it in a different light.

She clutches the doorjamb and licks her lips. "Tell me

the truth, Chase."

I nod, taking another deep breath.

I can't lie to her. Not anymore.

Nothing I do will rinse away all the bad I've done. All the evil that's seeped into my bones.

When I look at her, all I see is that birthmark on her neck … the image replaying in my mind over and over again. That mark is etched into my soul … and hers.

And she doesn't even know it's there.

Or what it really means.

I lower my head and rub my lips together. Deep down, I know I have to tell her. If I want her love and trust, then I need to be honest. No matter how badly it's going to hurt.

"Please …" Her pleading voice is my undoing. "I need to know what happened to my mother. How is she involved in this?"

It's time. "Did you know you have birthmark on your neck?" I ask.

She immediately touches it. "What does that have to do with this?"

"*Everything*," I reply. "Just tell me if you know."

"I think … A friend told me about it a long time ago, but it never bothers me."

I sigh, almost unable to say the words out loud.

"What?" she asks, approaching me. "What aren't you telling me, Chase?"

I can't even bear to look at her, knowing what I've known all along. I chose to hide it from her out of sheer selfishness. But I can't do it any longer.

She has to know, even if it means she'll leave me for it.

"It was ... the same birthmark your mother had."

She sucks in a breath and stops moving entirely.

I glance at her, forcing myself to look her in the face as I tell her the truth. "After you and I had sex, I found out it was the same one. I recognized it, so I went to Graham immediately."

She puts her hand in front of her mouth. "So I do have a mother? She's alive?" She grabs my arm. "Tell me about her. Tell me everything. How do you know her? And what does Graham have to do with it? Can I ... see her?"

I shake my head, licking my lips. "I'm sorry ... She's no longer—"

"No," she says, tears welling up in her eyes again. "Please tell me it isn't true."

"It is."

"Why? Why are you doing this now?" She vehemently shakes her head, like her heart is already breaking ... and so is mine when I look at her.

But I can't falter now. "Because I *need* to be honest with you. For once."

"What happened to her?" she screams.

It shatters what remains of my resolve.

"She ... she *died* because of me."

***

Syrena

"Wha …?" I can't even get the words out of my mouth.

My throat has completely clamped up, unable to even let out a breath.

"I didn't know you were hers," he says, but it doesn't make any sense in my mind.

What is this? What is happening?

Why does it feel as if my world just shifted on its axis?

"You knew her … and you *killed* her?" I mutter, the words reverberating in my ears.

My heart feels heavy, and my body so dizzy I almost fall, but he catches me. But feeling his arms around me is like poison to my skin right now, and I push him away.

"Let go of me," I snap.

I push past him and stumble into the living room naked.

"Let me explain, please," he says as I stumble toward my room.

"No," I reply coldly.

I need to put on clothes. Need to have something on me because I don't want him looking at me like … like he owns me. Like he has a right to see me.

Because he doesn't.

If what he said is true, he has no right to even touch me.

"Syrena …" He followed me.

So I turn around after putting on a simple dress and yell, "What did you do to her?"

"She …" He sighs. "She was Graham's captive. Just like you and Ella, except it was years ago."

I swallow away the lump in my throat at hearing his words because they don't really register even though they should. It feels so unreal.

"Years ago, he kept her to make babies … to sell. But after a while, it stopped working. Her mind and body couldn't cope. He lost his shit and sold her."

I shake my head, not wanting to believe this as the truth. It's too heinous, too despicable… and he's talking about … *my* mother?

"I was the one who bought her."

In shock, I take a step back. "What?"

"I wanted someone for my own. Someone who would never, ever question what I do. The killings. I needed someone who'd never tell a soul. Someone who I could … someday come to love."

What is he trying to say?

His footsteps come closer, so I back away again. "But there was a problem that I hadn't foreseen. When I bought her, she was already pregnant … with you."

"What?" I mutter, not knowing what to say.

"She carried her secret for months, not allowing anyone to come close, not even me. We didn't tell a soul. When you were born, she made me promise I would take care of you. But I didn't know she'd run straight back to him the day after."

"No." Clenching my jaw, I shake my head. "She wouldn't do that."

"He had her under his thumb, Syrena. Like a puppet. Nothing I did could sway her. Nothing."

"Don't …" I bury my face in my hands. "My mother wouldn't do that. She wouldn't leave me."

"She did, and I'm sorry," he says. "When he found out she'd given birth, she wouldn't tell him where his child was, which is when he—"

"Stop!" I shout, not wanting to hear it.

"You *have* to know. She loved you."

"No." Tears well up in my eyes. What mother would give up her child like that? What mother would run right back into the arms of the man who hurt her? Used her? Betrayed her?

"I … I should've kept an eye on her. Should've done more, anything, to make her stay."

"Please," I mutter. His words undo me. Strip me of all that makes me human and leave a scrambled set of bones scattered on the ground. That's how broken I feel.

"I was left … with you," he says. "And when I looked at you, I could see your mother's eyes reflect back at me. It killed me. So I … I …" He chokes on his own words. "I brought you to the hospital and left you there."

He sniffs. I can hear him cry, but it's not registering.

"I never knew Graham would find you again one day. Never imagined you two would ever cross paths."

"Lies," I hiss, overcome with fury.

"It's the truth. I didn't even know you were hers until I saw that birthmark."

"That's why you ran off …"

"Yes. I went straight to Graham to confront him about it. He admitted to you being hers… and his."

A shock ripples through me.

I hadn't even considered it up until now.

Graham … my father?

"No." I shake my head again. "It can't be true."

"It's the only truth I've ever kept from you."

"Why?" I shout.

"Because I didn't want you to get hurt," he says.

"But that sadistic fuck *can't* be my father! He just can't!" I feel unsteady, so I grab the table to keep myself from falling over.

"I didn't want to believe it either, but it's the truth. He just didn't care. That's why he wanted to sell you again."

My lips part, but nothing comes out. I'm left gasping for breath, trying to understand how this could happen to me. How I could be the product of that … monstrous man. And that even knowing all that, he still chose to sell me.

I want to kill him with my own bare hands.

"Is he still at the compound?" I say through gritted teeth.

"I know what you're thinking, and don't go there," Chase says. "I'll take care of it."

"Did you kill him?" I ask.

"I tried … but I failed." His voice sounds guttural. "But don't you even think about it, Syrena."

I am, but I can't stop thinking about everything else he told me either.

About how my life, even before my imprisonment in a cage, has been one giant lie.

I was always told my mother would come to pick me up some time. I even left the teddy bear at the orphanage, so she'd know I was still waiting for her. I kept going back there, time and time again, asking if someone had come for me.

But she never would.

My mother never cared enough because she didn't care to stay alive.

And Chase … never cared enough to force her to stay.

My fists clench as I raise my head high.

"I will go there and kill him myself if that makes it easier for you," he says. "If it will allow you to … forgive me."

How can I say no to that? Still, I can't bring myself to give him an answer. Because I don't want to forgive him.

"I know you're mad at me for leaving you at a hospital, but what else was I supposed to do? You know who I am, what I'm capable of. I wanted the best for you, and I knew I could never give that to you," he says.

I take a deep breath to try to focus, but my mind is buzzing with information, overwhelmed with trying to process everything.

"Please, Syrena … you have to believe me," he adds, his

voice soft and drenched in fear.

I shake my head. Nothing he says matters. Nothing can fix what he's done.

He lied to me, kept this from me, when he knew all this time who I was.

He knew my mother while I never had the chance ... and now it's all gone because of him.

"I'm sorry ..." he says, the sound of defeat echoing in his voice. "I understand if you hate me now."

"I do," I say. It hurts. Like a bullet grazing my heart. But I can't feel anything except pain right now ... and that pain is worse than anything he could ever do to me.

"Let me out," I say resolutely.

He doesn't respond.

It's the only thing he's tried to prevent me from doing. His one weakness. *Me.*

Because that's what this was all about. Keeping me under lock and key. Forcing me to be with him. But I can't do it any longer. I can't stay with the man who caused my life to be a miserable hell.

"Open the door," I say.

"It is open," he replies. "I never locked it."

I take a breath and swallow it down. Did he know this would happen? Did he plan on telling me all this, knowing I'd leave in the end?

I don't ask. Right now, that knowledge will only make this decision harder.

Instead, I march toward the door. When I smell his

cologne, I pause.

"I won't stop you," he says.

"Why now?" I ask.

"Because ... I trust you," he says, swallowing. "And I want you to be happy, even if that means being somewhere else. Even if it means you'll turn me in. It doesn't matter anymore. Do what you want to do. Be free."

His words sound fragile, painful even, but I can't let it get to me.

"Thank you," I reply, unsure of what to say or even how to feel.

He never even considered letting me out before. But I guess some things are too hard to take, even for him. He knows this final admission broke me.

But I won't let his trust be in vain. I owe him that much for finally telling me the truth.

He doesn't block my way as he stands in the hallway. I pass him without saying goodbye.

How could one ever say goodbye after learning all that?

Impossible.

So I strut out the door with my head held high, feeling the overwhelming weight of the outside world on my shoulders, but I relent.

TWENTY-FOUR

Syrena

A few weeks later

"You left a spot here," Roy says, clenching his teeth. "I give you a place to sleep and work after you disappeared on me for months, and this is how you do your job?"

He chucks the towel at my face.

"Sorry," I say, grabbing it and quickly dabbing the table again.

"Don't do it again," he grumbles as he shuffles off.

I'm trying my best not to throw the towel right back at him, but I have to keep my composure. Roy's club is the only place with a decent room for me. None of the motels would take me without a credit card, and some even threatened to call the cops on me. So what else was I supposed to do but come right back to the only place I know that will accept me?

I just have to ignore the constant moaning of the girls fucking the customers in the back of the club as I clean the tables and throw away the dirty water from my bucket.

When I'm finally done cleaning, I go upstairs for a little bit to have lunch. Roy gives me a small paycheck off which I can at least survive. It's not much, but it's something.

Still, sitting here on my bed, slurping up noodles from a cup, I can't help but think back to the warm bed and comfortable home I lived in for what felt like an eternity. I choke up a little and cough as tears spring to my eyes.

Even though it didn't last long, it was the most illuminating time in my life.

And maybe even … the best I've ever had. Just remembering Chase's food makes my mouth water as I pretend he made these noodles.

Goddammit, I really have to stop doing this every time I eat.

Or shower.

Or lie in bed.

But for some reason, my mind can't stop drifting off to that man who consumed my every waking thought. Who gave me all the riches in the world and never wanted anything in return except love. Whose only weakness was his lust for power … and his need to kill those who stood in the way.

A shiver runs up and down my spine, and I sniff to stop myself from crying. I can't. Not over him. It's because of him that I lost a shot at a proper life. If he hadn't let my mom escape, if he hadn't let her run back to Graham—my fucking father—she would've been alive to take care of me.

She would've done anything to protect me. To nurture me. To help me. Right?

That's what I keep telling myself, but then why did she leave me with him? I was only a little baby. And just to go back to that ... monster?

I throw the empty cup of noodles into the corner of my room and huddle on my bed with my blanket wrapped firmly around me. I can't believe that sick bastard, Graham, is really my father.

I refuse to even call him that.

Did he know when he took me from this very club that I was his daughter?

Or was it all a fluke? A random chance meeting?

Was I just some blind girl without a past he could easily lock up and use?

I shake my head. I'll never know the answers—not until I talk to him, and that's never going to happen because I'm never, ever going back to the compound.

I just have to figure out a way to contact Ella and Cage. Maybe if I save enough money, I can hire someone to get them out of there. If I can ever even figure out where the hell the compound is.

God, I don't think I've ever hated being blind more than today.

"Syrena? Get your ass down here. The customers need more drinks!" Roy shouts, banging on the door.

I sigh and get out from my curled-up ball. I'm not ready to face the noise downstairs, the clapping and whistling customers, the loud music, Roy's yelling.

But I go anyway.

I go because I must.

Because this is the life I chose.

The freedom I so desperately wanted.

***

CHASE

A few days later

As I sit on the stool and stare at the dark wall ahead of me, I fade away into oblivion.

I don't think I've ever gotten so drunk before that I don't even know what I'm doing, but I don't care. Alcohol is the only thing that'll drown out her voice. Her whispers. Her touch.

But fuck me … I can't stop thinking about her.

She's probably at Roy's right now, working her ass off for a meager paycheck. That fucker can't see what she's worth, doesn't know what he has.

What if he hits her again?

Just the thought makes my blood boil.

I should go there and get her, but I know she'd hate me for it, which is the last thing I want. I'm going against every fiber of my being by not helping her. I didn't even give her cash so she could stay at a better place than Roy's, but I know she'll never accept it. Not even when I forced it on her. She'd just chuck it back in my face.

She doesn't want me anymore. Or anything that has to do with me.

I take another sip and stare wistfully at the people around me, wondering if they're here for the very same reason I am. If they're drowning in a hell of their own making too. If one of them is a delinquent … because if so, I might kill that one later.

I really need a fix right now.

Anything to get rid of this rage flowing through my veins.

Fuck, I should've killed Graham when I had the chance.

Way back when … when I first got my hands on her mother. I should've finished the job then. But no, I actually wanted to let him continue, so I could catch more of the guys who continuously went to him to get *their* fix. I wanted all of them to die so badly that I exchanged my own morals for the sake of hunting them down. I'm just as evil as they are.

Fuck, I need more to drink.

I slurp up the whiskey and slam down my glass onto the bar. "Another one."

Suddenly, someone sits down beside me and holds his hand over my glass. "Enough." I look up into Brandon's familiar face. "Don't you think?"

"Oh … it's you again," I say.

"Hello to you too," he says, laughing. "You look like a mess."

"Thanks, so do you."

"Hey, you invited me here, remember?"

"Did I?" I narrow my eyes. "Can't remember."

He nods. "Figured." He signals the bartender. "Two waters, please."

"Water?" I scoff. "What kind of pussy are you?"

"The pussy who helps his friend when he's obviously in need."

"Tsk …" I grumble, looking away. "I don't need any help."

"Right." He slides one of the glasses filled with water toward me. "Drink up. Might make you feel better."

Reluctantly, I take a big gulp, but it doesn't do it for me.

"What are you doing here?" he asks after a while.

"What does it look like?" I glance his way.

"Like you're trying to kill yourself."

I shrug. "Not sure if that's so bad."

"No." He grabs my shoulders and forces me to turn around. "But the you I know would *never* say this."

"Maybe the world is better off without me. Don't you

think?"

He raises a brow. "What's gotten into you?"

"Nothing," I reply, completely blanking out. "Have another name on the list? I could do with a hit."

"Stop," he says, briefly placing a hand on my shoulder. "That's enough."

"Why?" I frown.

"Because you're clearly miserable. Why?"

"Because she's gone, that's why." I turn my head so I don't have to see the obnoxious look on his face. I know he thinks I'm a sad, pathetic asshole, and he's right. But I don't need confirmation of that right now. I know exactly who I am and what I've done.

"What, did she escape?" he scoffs.

I let out a sigh and put down my glass. "I let her go."

There's an uncomfortable silence, and for a second, I think he might've run off.

"What? For real?" There's more shock in his voice than I anticipated.

I nod, and he pats me on the back. "Well done."

I gaze his way. "I told her everything."

His eyes widen. "*Everything* everything?"

"*Everything.*" I take another sip of water just to cope with that thought.

"Even the ki—"

"Even that," I interrupt.

"But why?"

"Because she deserved to know *everything.*"

"And you trust her with all that information?" he asks.

"With my life," I say. "And if she calls the cops ... well, I don't even care."

He coughs. "Would she, though?"

"You never know." I shrug. "Not that it matters."

"Right." He nods slowly. "Well, whatever reasons you had for telling her and then releasing her ... I'm still proud of you."

"Oh, save it," I groan, finishing my drink. "Another one!" I call out to the bartender.

"You should be proud of yourself too. You did something not even you considered a possibility."

"And I lost *her* in the process."

"You didn't let her go freely?"

"She demanded to be let out. How could I not oblige?" I say with a deadly grin, which disappears instantly because it was meaningless. Just like my life.

"You gave her what she wanted," he says. It's not a question.

"Yep," I say, drawing circles on the wood with just my index finger while trying not to lose my mind.

It's quiet for some time again, and we both drink our water in peace. It doesn't quite match up to the alcohol from before, but I get what he's doing. He's trying to keep me alive, and I appreciate that even though I don't see the point.

"You're not going to leave me alone, are you?" I ask.

"Nope."

I shake my head, snorting.

Of course, that's the kind of friend he is. Never let down someone in need. Even when he hates you for it.

But what about her? Did I let her down in need? Or did I finally give her what she needed the most? Even if she hates me for it?

I wonder where she is right now. If she's doing what she's always wanted. If she's happy.

If she can feel only a fragment more than what she felt when she was with me, then that's enough for me.

I can live with her not being near me as long as she's alive.

As long as she finds what she's looking for in life.

Because I'll never find it again. That, I'm sure of.

It was only when I lost her that I realized just how much she really meant to me. How much she's seeped into my soul and still lingers there.

I love her.

And that's why I let her go.

"If it's killing you that much, why didn't you convince her to stay?" Brandon asks.

I slam my fist on the bar. "Don't you think I tried?"

Now everyone's looking at me. I clear my throat and add, "Sorry." And we wait until everyone in the room settles down again.

"I'll never see her again …" I mutter, gazing at the glass of water in front of me.

"Not if you don't try to win her back," Brandon says.

I snort. "Win her back? After everything I said?"

"Why not? If you love her ... And you clearly do, looking at how fucked up you are right now."

I shake my head, but when I open my mouth, I can't think of the words to say to refute him.

Because that's just the thing ... I can't.

He's absolutely right.

But is that really what I should do?

It's selfish. Arrogant.

I'm an asshole to think she'd ever want me to come get her. To ever think I deserve her in my life.

"No. She doesn't want me."

"How do you know?"

"You didn't see the look on her face when I told her," I say.

"I don't have to. Can you see inside her mind? Maybe she was just upset. Obviously. But how do you know she doesn't love you too?"

"How could anyone love a monster like me?" I say, frowning.

"How do you know they *can't?*"

My lips part, but I grab the water and chug that down instead. "Goddammit."

Brandon laughs. "Not everything has to be so complicated. Stop making up excuses. Just try ..."

"And then what?" I growl.

He shrugs. "If she doesn't, you'll figure it out. But you have to at least give it a shot. Fight for her. Maybe it'll work, you never know." He smiles. "Besides, she's had a taste of freedom now. She got what she wanted. I don't think she'll lie to you. There's no need if you let her make her own decision."

"Right." I slurp down the water in one go.

"If she knows who you are … what you are … and she still accepted you … then why not?"

He makes it seem so simple, and as I nod at his words, I come to realize that it truly is that simple.

Love isn't about questions and answers, about truths and lies, or about rights and wrongs.

It's about how badly you want it more than anything. How crippled it makes you feel when it isn't there. And how powerful it makes you feel when it is.

Because when she was in my arms … I felt impenetrable.

Like I was always going to be there to protect her. Like she could take anything she wanted from me, and I'd still have enough to give.

I slam the glass on the bar and get up from the stool.

"Where are you going?" Brandon asks.

As I glance over my shoulder, I grin and say, "To fight."

TWENTY-FIVE

Syrena

At night, I'm cleaning up the tables as usual while all the other waitresses have already left. Even Roy's already left, as he expects me to take care of the inside and close up the club. Usually, it takes me until three in the morning to get things done, but there were fewer customers tonight, so it's less filthy than normal.

When I'm done washing all the glasses and sweeping the floor, I grab the keys from the kitchen counter and walk to the door.

However, the moment I'm there, it opens right in front of me, and a familiar voice breaks my train of thought.

"Syrena."

I hold my breath and take a step back, clenching the keys in my hand.

Is this real? Is he really here?

I must be dreaming.

I shake my head.

"How are you?"

There's that voice again ... it's definitely his.

But why? I haven't seen him in weeks ... I don't even know how long. And now he's suddenly here? In the flesh?

"Wh-what are you doing here?" I ask, my voice unsteady, just as wobbly as my legs.

"I wanted to come see you." His voice is so soft, it unravels the part of my heart I thought I'd finally locked away again.

I hold the keys close to my chest. "How did you find me?"

"Roy's Strip Club. Not a name that's used often," he says, and I can actually hear him smirk. "Didn't take me long to track it down. And you."

Yet he chose not to come to take me ... until this day.

"Why now?" I ask.

"You know why." He closes the door behind him and steps closer.

"Don't," I mumble, holding up the keys like they're a knife, as if they'd provide any protection.

"I'm not here to hurt you," he says. "I promise."

For some reason, my hand instinctively lowers. As if it

knows I can trust him even when he's lied to my face many times before.

He did it to protect me.

Although I never asked for protection.

"You did it once … What's stopping you from trying to take me away again?" I say through gritted teeth, not allowing myself to show even an ounce of mercy.

Not because I can't … but because if I did, it would mean the end of my defense.

If he ever touches me again, I just know I wouldn't be able to resist. Wouldn't be able to deny my heart the thing it's craved for so long.

His touch is like a drug to me, and I just can't. I can't allow myself to go there.

"I didn't come here to force you to come home," he says.

"Then why did you come?" I say, licking my lips.

"To give you information about Cage and Ella."

My breathing stops momentarily, and I grab the chair next to me for support. "Are they alive?"

"Yes. We've managed to track them down."

"Oh, thank God," I mutter, breathing out a sigh of relief.

"I've written down the address for you. If you have a phone, you can let it read it out loud for you with an app."

"Okay." I frown. "And what do you want in return?"

I assume he wants something. Men always do.

Nothing's ever free in this world.

"Nothing," he says.

My lips part, but I don't know what to say. That was ... unexpected.

"So ... Roy's Strip Club," he says, his voice dark. "Is he treating you better than before?"

I mull it over for a second. "Well, he doesn't hit me, if that's what you're asking."

"Good. If he ever puts his hands on you again and I find out, I will kill him."

Not a single ounce of hesitation lingers in his voice.

It must be hard for him knowing I came back to the very man who treated me so badly, but he must understand that I had no other choice.

It was this ... or back to *him*.

And still, he demands nothing of me. Doesn't force me to come back with him even though I can tell from his voice alone he almost wants to beg me.

It's a strength I can only admire.

"Here," Chase says, handing the small paper to me.

I quickly take it and tuck it into my pocket before he can take it away again.

"There's something I have to add, though ..." He clears his throat. "You have another brother."

"Another brother?" I say, flabbergasted.

"His name is Lock. He escaped the compound long before Ella and Cage did. Much older too. Apparently, he lived on an island by himself for quite some time. That's all my contacts managed to find out."

"Whoa." I swallow away the lump in my throat. "And you're sure they're … my family?"

"Hundred percent. Graham admitted it himself. You're his."

I can't keep my legs steady any longer, so I grab the chair and sit down on it.

I can't believe it.

I actually have a family.

Not one … but two brothers.

"Ella and Cage also have a kid together," Chase adds casually. "Thought you should know."

And a niece or nephew too. Holy shit.

"I know it's a lot to take in, so take your time," he says, taking a deep breath.

I nod a few times, but then he pushes something soft into my hands.

"I also wanted to give you this," he says.

But I'm not listening to his words. All I can do is touch the soft, squishy stuffed animal in my hands. My teddy bear.

"You left it at the orphanage." I can hear him smile. "Thought you'd want it back."

"But I never told you," I mutter, flabbergasted.

"You didn't have to." I can hear him smile. "I'm the one who gave it to you."

My heart shatters into tiny pieces.

This teddy bear didn't belong to my mother?

It came from him?

My whole body trembles as Chase keeps flipping my

world upside down again and again.

All this time, I was searching for a home. A place to call my own. Someone who would come and get me and pull me from the darkness.

And all this time, it turned out to be him.

It was always him.

"Well, that's all I came to do," he says.

Then he turns around and walks off.

"Wait," I say.

I don't know why I say it. Maybe I really don't want him to leave.

A part of me wishes this whole conversation never happened because then I'd be able to continue working like a braindead person as I normally do, not giving a shit about what happens to the rest of the world.

But another part of me desperately needed this little push. This little shot of happiness straight into my veins. And a part of me carelessly needed to see him.

Even if it meant breaking my own heart all over again.

He stops in his tracks but doesn't say a word.

The pause seems eternal before I speak up and finally make up my mind. "Why did you tell me all that and give me this? Just to leave again?"

"Because I meant what I said. I love you so much that I want nothing more than for you to be happy," he says. "Even if that means letting you go."

He continues walking. Just like that.

As if he didn't just rip my heart out of my chest and take

it with him, all the way to the door, all the way to the car, until the sound of his engine drifts out of range, and I can no longer call for him to stay.

That moment's passed.

Just like our time together.

So short yet so significant.

It changed my life.

And I never even told him how grateful I am for this information that's about to alter my life again.

Where I'll finally be reunited with the people I shared so much with. Where I'll finally meet ... my family.

And it's all thanks to him.

TWENTY-SIX

CHASE

A week later

I stare at the coffee in my cup, watching it ripple as someone places a laptop on the table. The people around me are talking so loud, it gives me a headache, and I try not to pay attention even though I should.

My mind just isn't in the right space for a meeting right now. I'm just here because I should be, not because I want to. I'm literally holding myself back from walking right out of that door … and going on a killing spree.

That's how far down the gutter I've gone.

I don't know how much longer I can stop myself from giving into my urges, but I don't want to be that man anymore. I don't want to be the man who she feared.

Syrena … Fuck.

I miss her so badly it hurts my body.

My heart feels tight and constricted in my chest as I chew on my lip. Not a second in the day goes by when I don't think about her, wondering if she's still in that same bar, if she's already seen her friends. If she's still happy.

Happiness … It's the only thing that keeps me from going to her.

Because I know I've only stolen it away from her.

What have I ever given her except complete devastation?

I frown, still staring at the coffee, which has probably gone cold by now.

I don't deserve her. I never did.

I'm a beast who only lives to kill. She could never love a man like me.

For my sake, and hers, I have to stop being that monster. I have to stop randomly killing criminals just to get a fix.

She'd want it that way … I think.

I don't think I ever really knew what she truly wanted.

All I know is that this is for the best.

"Chase?"

A voice in the corner of the room makes me lift my head, but I have no clue who's calling me or what they want from me. I didn't catch the question. I haven't paid any attention to the meeting whatsoever since I came here.

"Sorry, what?" I ask.

"Are you okay?" the chairman asks.

I swallow and sigh. "Yeah … I'm fine," I say, clearing my throat.

"You don't look fine," another one says. "Did you even hear what we said?"

"Yeah, this is an important topic," someone else says.

I shake my head. "I'm sorry, guys."

"Okay, how about this …" The chairman closes his folders for a second. "I suggest you go take care of whatever is on your mind first, and then we can all come back and get a fresh start on this. We're running out of options anyway, so it's good to take a break for a day and see if you can come up with anything new."

The other people in the meeting don't seem too happy about that decision, and it's as though it was made just for me, but I'm grateful.

"Thank you," I say.

The chairman nods as he packs up his things and leaves.

I quickly shake everyone's hand before walking out and going straight down to the parking garage.

He's right. I do need to get my mind off things. Or rather … her.

If I don't do something quickly, I fear I might succumb to killing just to sate my needs… to fill the hole she's left. Maybe it makes more sense than keeping it all tucked inside. I'm like a walking bomb ready to explode, and I don't like it one bit.

I drive home with knots in my stomach, trying to figure out if I should call Brandon. The phone's right beside me on the passenger's seat, and it's as if it's staring straight back at me, whispering in my ear to make that call.

And even though I so desperately want to rid myself of this annoyance, I resist the urge to pick it up until I get home, where I quickly tuck it into my pocket without looking at the missed calls.

I can't give in. I just can't. I have to do this. For me. For her.

To prove that I'm capable of more than doing evil.

That I can live … without her. And that I won't ruin myself in the process.

As I open the door and take off my coat, I stop dead in my tracks.

In the middle of the living room is—

"Syrena?" I mutter.

Am I dreaming?

I must be. A hallucination of some sort because I'm so goddamn addicted to her.

"Hi."

Her voice. It's definitely her.

She's really here.

My lips part, but I have no clue what to say.

Why is she here? And how?

A noise in the kitchen immediately makes me turn my head and peer around the corner. Someone throws a knife in the sink. A muffled voice speaks up.

"Sorry 'bout that."

Brandon walks out with a sandwich stuffed in his mouth. "I got hungry, so I made a PB and J. Hope you don't mind."

I frown, shaking my head, still not knowing what to say to all this.

He grabs my shoulder and whispers, "I was just coming over to check on you, but then I found her sitting in front of your door, so I let her in." He takes a bite of his sandwich. "Also, just wanted to let you know I saved the other girl."

My eyes widen. "On your own?"

He shrugs and then winks. "Yeah. Problem?"

I mull it over for a second.

We were going to save them all together, that was the agreement, but I guess I slipped up along the way, and Brandon took care of it. Even though I'm pissed as hell he'd go on a killing spree and be the hero without me, I can't be mad at him for doing the right thing.

I sigh. "Well done."

The smirk on his face is almost as irritating as the amount of noise he makes when he chews. "You're welcome," he says. When everything's still silent, he adds, "Well, I'll leave you two to it then."

As he walks out the door, I mutter, "Thanks." But I don't think he heard.

All I can do is gaze at the girl in front of me ... and the beautiful, independent woman she's transformed into.

I still can't believe she's truly here in the flesh, right in front of me.

I thought I'd never see her again. Swore to myself I'd never go to the place she works at ever again. Not for my sake, but for hers. Because that was what she needed … her own life, without me.

Yet here she is, in my home, stepping closer, while my body feels frozen to the ground.

"Are you really here?" I mutter, shaking my head.

"Yes," she replies.

"But why?" I can barely utter the words.

"Because …" She licks her lips. "I didn't have the chance to say thank you." She swallows. "For the address. And the bear."

I smile softly. "You don't have to. I don't need a thank you," I reply. "I don't even deserve it."

"Yes, you do," she says, taking another step. "You gave them to me out of your own free will. I didn't ask you to, and you still gave the address to me without asking for anything in return."

"Because I want you to be happy," I say.

"I know," she says, nodding. "But—"

"Don't," I interrupt.

I don't want her to say this because she feels like she needs to or because she thinks I'm unhappy. I'm not. I'm happy as long as she is, and I refuse to give in to my weakness. "You don't have to do this," I say.

"But I want to," she says.

"You don't have to forgive me. You don't have to thank

me. I know what I did. And I know I can never give back what I took from you."

"That's not why I'm here," she says.

"Then why are you?" My heart feels heavy. I'm so goddamn close to bursting. I want to shout, scream, punch holes in the walls … and then kiss her. Madly. Deeply.

But I force myself to stay put. To stay where I'm supposed to be … away from her.

I'll only ruin her.

"I realized something when I was working at Roy's," she says, her eyes tearing up. "No matter how much I hate you for what you did to me, for what happened to my mother … I can't stop wanting you either."

My knees buckle, and I fall to the floor. I can't even look her in the eyes. Can't bear the weight that's on my shoulders any longer.

"Even though you caused all the pain and misery in my life, you didn't do it to hurt me."

"But I did …" I growl, planting my hands firmly on the floor so I don't use them to get back up on my feet again.

"You didn't know what my mother would do," she says.

"But I could've stopped her!"

"Guilt eats you up. I can sense it." She steps even closer. "Is that why you gave me freedom? Because it killed you to see me in pain, knowing you were the cause?"

"Yes." Just admitting it feels painful. That single word rolling off my tongue feels like an ocean wave crashing into me.

"You tried to do anything you could to make things up to me," she says. She's right in front of me now. I could almost touch her, but I refuse to let myself. "You just wanted to prove to yourself that you weren't a bad man, even after everything you did."

"I failed," I say.

Suddenly, she grabs my face and lifts it, forcing me to look at her. To gaze at all the beauty she is … and how little of it I deserve.

"In your twisted little way, you wanted to make the world better. You wanted it to be better for me." Her warm hands cupping my face are like those of an angel. "And the longer I thought about it, the less I could stop wanting to come back here."

"I can't give you what you need," I mutter.

"Yes, you can. You already did … time and time again."

"I'm a killer. A monster. Someone who takes and takes without giving back. How could you ever want a man like that?" I say.

"I can't explain it either. I just know that I do," she says.

"I can't change who I am, Syrena." I grab both her hands and hold them close to my heart, forcing her to feel the real me. "This is it. This is me."

"And I accept that," she says without an ounce of regret. "I'm not afraid of you. Not afraid of the monster inside you … because I know he'll never hurt me."

My lips part, but I have no words.

"And I forgive you for what you've done."

Her final words unravel me. Unchain my heart and set it free.

And as I raise my head, I fall into her, wrapping my arms so tightly around her body I feel like she's going to pop. But it doesn't matter. She doesn't say a word, so I know she doesn't mind. And when she places her hand on my back, I can finally breathe.

She's here in my arms.

She's here to stay.

Here …

Mine.

I grab her face and smash my lips onto hers, not giving a shit about whether it's wrong or right, or any of that bullshit.

When I kiss her, all the noise in my head seems to disappear.

All that remains is her. It's always been her.

From the moment I met her to the point when I had to let her go … I knew she was the one. The only one to ever understand what it's like to feel as though you're an outsider in your own life. To feel as if you're an outcast. To want something that's depraved … And to give in to it anyway, knowing you'll go to hell for it.

I want her, need her, so badly that I can't stop claiming her mouth, pulling her down with me to the ground.

She kneels in front of me and lets me part her lips with my tongue as I desperately want to get closer.

My hands can't stop touching her; my tongue can't stop tasting her.

I'm addicted to the ruin that is us …

Addicted to the warmth she injects in my veins, filling me with the hope that I can be a better person.

For her.

I can do it all.

TWENTY-SEVEN

Syrena

I know what I did. I know damn right what I unleashed when I made the decision to come back to him.

But I couldn't stop myself. I couldn't force myself to stay in a place I really didn't want to be. I only did it because I thought it was the right thing to do … because of the pain I felt.

All that was just my head trying to make right what had gone wrong, but the thing with hearts is that they can't ever be fixed. Love isn't right or wrong, it isn't easy, and it's definitely not always healthy.

But this love is undeniable, unshakable, and I can't

ignore what my heart wants.

My need for him has only grown since I left, and when I finally got the chance to speak to him again, everything came pouring out of me. It was the honest truth. The only truth I've denied myself for so long.

I knew it the moment I first kissed him that this was more than just a means to an end.

He stole my heart and chained it to his body, and I can never get it back. No matter how hard we both tried to stay away from each other.

He ruined me … and I ruined him.

And if loving him means I'm just as evil as he is, then so be it.

I can live with knowing what he truly is … knowing that he once tried to kill me.

He couldn't.

And that's where our fates collided.

Where our hearts melted into one.

Where I was bound to him forever … even if I didn't know it yet.

I do know now. I know it all, and I accept every inch of responsibility that comes with loving a beast of a man. I have no regrets, whatsoever.

The longer he kisses me, the more I realize I finally made the right decision.

The game we played never was one about freedom or power … it was about our inevitable clash. Like magnets, we drew to each other until nothing was left but him and me.

Around him, I always feel naked. Stripped bare of everything that makes me, *me*. My past, my present, my future—all together as one. And it's okay. It's okay to be vulnerable. It's okay to be who I am around him because I'm no longer afraid.

And right now, I want nothing more than for him to hold me. Kiss me. Touch me everywhere, and more.

His kisses are feverish and desperate, as if he can't get close enough, even though I'm already in his arms. His presence surrounds me, towers over me, even on his knees, and I love how small it makes me feel. How when he takes what he wants from me, I feel freed.

He moans softly as his lips leave a trail of wetness all the way down my neck. I can sense his agony and how much he's yearned for me in the way he kisses me. It's been so long … too long.

And as my head tilts back, his teeth sink into my shoulder.

I don't feel the pain. Only the pleasure.

And when he laps up the small trickle of blood, I moan along with him.

It's bliss.

His hands grasp my breast, squeezing straight through the fabric. His breathing becomes more erratic, his kisses more temperamental as my nipples peak under his fingers. He groans out loud and then tears away my shirt. Ripping it through the middle, he makes me squeal. Within seconds, it's gone, thrown halfway across the room, and his mouth is all over me, leaving tantalizing licks and kisses wherever he goes.

"I can't control myself," he whispers against my skin.

"Then don't," I murmur, gasping when he sucks on my nipple.

"God … What did I ever do to deserve you," he murmurs.

I smile and reach for his pants, unzipping them quickly and pulling out his cock. He's already hard, bouncing up and down, pre-cum dripping from the tip. As I start to massage him, he rocks along with my movements, groaning like an animal.

His grip on my nipples only tightens, but the sizzling pain feels amazing, and I want nothing more than for him to take me right now.

It's as if he can sense exactly what I need because his fingers immediately dive underneath my skirt and slide up my thighs. When they reach my panties, he briefly caresses me, making me crave him even more. Then he harshly rips away the fabric, and I cry out in surprise.

"Don't say I never warned you," he growls.

I chuckle, but I'm immediately interrupted by his lips smashing onto mine.

He claims both my mouth and my pussy as his, sliding his fingers up and down my slit. He moans into my mouth, a wicked smirk spreading on his lips. "You're already wet. Miss me that much?"

I nod, but then he captures my mouth once more, and

I'm lost in desire again.

His tongue expertly twirls around mine as his fingers toy with me, and I can barely keep my hands steady as I palm him. His impressive length still makes my mouth water, still makes me want to beg.

But I don't even have to because he's already one step ahead of me, pushing me down onto the floor with simple kisses and greedy touches. He's right on top of me, fondling me, shoving his fingers up into my pussy as if he owns it. And he does. He owns every inch of my soul.

For this exact reason, I can never escape him. Even if he lets me leave, I could never turn my back. Not on this. Not on *him*.

"Fuck, I need you," he says through ragged breaths. "I need to feel you."

"Fuck me," I say as he pulls my hands above my head in a vise grip. He pauses, and his hand twitches. I say it again. "Fuck me."

The louder the words, the tighter his hand pushes down my wrists. I love how it feels. Love the way he turns into a savage beast.

He grunts and shoves my skirt up even farther, parting my legs as he positions himself on top of me. "Oh, I'm going to fuck you all right."

"Yes," I moan as his tip enters me.

"Hard," he adds.

"Yes …" I mewl as he thrusts in.

"Fast."

I gasp as he pulls out and buries himself deep inside me again.

He grabs my face and smashes his lips on mine, fucking me into oblivion. And I'm loving every second of it; my mind completely wasted on lust.

"I can't be gentle, Syrena," he whispers, nibbling on my lip.

"I want you … Chase," I murmur as his fingers twist my nipples, making it hard to breathe.

"You want the monster?" he asks.

Suddenly, he slaps my breast, making me squeal, then rams his cock inside me while I do.

"Say it!"

"I want you," I say. "Give me the monster."

"How long? One fuck?" he asks as he thrusts into me. "One night? One week?"

"Forever."

He pauses and leans over to caress my cheek. Then he grasps my chin. "Is this your choice?"

I don't even need to think about it. That's how certain I am. I don't even care what happened. All I care about is him being with me … inside me.

"Yes," I reply.

The admittance feels like a breath of relief.

He smiles and gives me a peck on the lips. "Good …" he groans, fucking me even harder. "Because I'm not letting you escape ever again."

He leans up and slides back inside my pussy. I can feel

his length bumping inside me, the feeling like heavenly sin. I moan with each thrust, my body covered in goose bumps, deliciously rippling with heat.

His hand lowers from my chin to my neck, carefully sliding his fingers down so I can feel every inch of them … and then he wraps them around my throat. All while still fucking me madly.

"Are you afraid?" he asks.

I shake my head.

I know he won't hurt me.

He loves me too much, needs me too much to ever risk it.

His fingers tighten, and still, I don't feel anything but the need for him to go beyond what both of us thought was possible. I want to give him my all, even if it means handing over my life.

With him, I just know I'm safe.

I just know.

Our bond goes deeper than skin. Deeper than any pain anyone could ever inflict on me.

And this? Him holding me down like some kind of pet? This doesn't feel like a threat.

It feels like an invitation.

A game to see if I'm willing to let myself go for his needs.

And I am.

This is all a power play. It's something he craves, something I can give.

So I let him push me to my limits as he fucks me on the floor until I'm almost out of breath.

Then he releases me, and I suck in air, only for him to wrap his fingers around my neck again. I focus on the smell of hot sex, the sound of his animalistic moans, and the feel of his balls slapping against my skin.

And as he comes, so do I.

Right as his fingers practically choke me, my pussy begins to thump, and an explosion of orgasmic proportions builds up through my body. His thrusts stop deep inside me as his cum jets into me, accompanied by a roar that sounds like euphoria to me.

His fingers release the pressure as he plants his hands beside my head, hovering close to my lips. "Did I hurt you?"

I grin and chuckle.

"Is that good or bad?" he adds.

"Good," I mutter. "Definitely good."

He hums with amusement and says, "That's what I like to hear."

I smile, but the realization kicks in that the healing process has only just begun.

I want to erase the bad memories and replace them with new ones. Better ones.

I swallow away the lump in my throat. "Collar me."

"What?" he says, confusion lacing his voice.

"Make me yours."

The silence seems to last forever, but I know he heard.

Suddenly, he pulls us both up from the floor, carrying

me all the way back into that same room I was in before. *My* room.

But this time, it doesn't feel like a prison as he slams the door shut with his foot and puts me down on the floor. It only takes him a second to find the metal that instantly reminds me of what I've been through, but this time, it no longer sends me into a panic.

Instead, I'm calm and needy for more. More of him. More of everything.

And when the familiar metal wraps itself around my throat and clings into place, I don't feel as if I've been robbed of my freedom. Instead, the chain in his hands as he tugs me toward him feels like power. Feels like more freedom than I've ever had before.

"You don't have to do this," he says.

I place my hand on his cheek and say, "Yes, I do."

"I can live without it," he mutters.

"No, you can't," I reply. "And neither can I."

I can feel his smile forming underneath the tip of my fingers.

His forehead leans against mine as he slowly inches closer and kisses me—fully, honestly—as only a man could. He's not just a monster or a beast. He's a man too. My man. Only this man could give me so much by taking away everything I have.

And right now, I don't want to be anywhere but here in his arms.

He shoves me against the door and lets his mouth roam

freely across my skin again. His hands fumble at my skirt, pulling it down until I'm completely naked in front of him, despite him being fully clothed. And I don't even mind one bit.

"God, I don't think I'll ever get tired of fucking your pretty body," he muses. "Or mouth."

"Take me. Take it all," I say.

"Any way I want?" he murmurs, sucking on my bottom lip.

I nod. "Anything."

He bites down ever so slightly until my lip cracks, and he licks up the blood gleefully.

Out of nowhere, he spins me around on my feet, planting me face-first against the door. The chain still firmly in his hand, he pulls back my head and whispers into my ear, "You know I like it rough."

His hand circles my ass.

SMACK!

My legs tremble, but the pain sizzles right down to my pussy, making me so damn wet again.

He massages my ass and does the same to the other cheek, giving both equal treatment until they're tingling, and my legs are wobbly. But his dick pushing into my thighs reminds me to stay awake.

He leans away toward the cabinet, and the next thing I know, something's squirted onto my ass.

"This might hurt a little … but you'll love it," he says, and then his fingers enter me from behind. Right in my ass.

"Because *I* do."

I gasp as he probes me, feels me, fills me up with just one finger ... and then he adds another one.

"So tight ... already whimpering," he murmurs.

"F-fuck," I mumble, not even able to pronounce more than one syllable.

I can hear him smile. "It's only going to get tighter ... and harder."

After pulling out, he swipes his length along my ass and then pushes inside, inch by inch. I hold my breath the entire way, my nails digging into the door.

"Take it like a good girl," he groans, pushing farther inside. "All the way."

I'm on my tiptoes as he fills me up completely. Fuck me. I never expected this to happen so soon again. Or for it to feel so good. So fucking ... full.

As he starts to move, I can feel it everywhere. In my ass, my legs, my pussy ... even my nipples harden as he thrusts. His cum is still dripping out of me as he buries himself inside my other hole, but I don't even mind. I'm wasted on lust. Wasted on him as he pulls the chain and forces me to tilt my head back.

God, I love how forceful he is.

Have I lost my mind? Maybe.

But I prefer it this way. I love surrendering to him because it frees me in ways I never thought possible. And the pleasure is more intense than anything I've ever experienced before.

It's as if he knows exactly how to play me, how to push my buttons to make me squeal and beg.

Still holding the chain with one hand, he moves his other hand between my legs. He claims my pussy by twisting my clit, rubbing it until I'm literally shaking with need. His cum mixes with my wetness, dripping down my legs as he thrusts into my ass.

Arousal peaks as I moan while he flicks me, the grip on the chain growing tighter and tighter. He uses it as reins. Reins to fuck me—to control my body—and I'm letting him.

And as he comes, roaring out loud once again, I do too. His fingers thrum to the rhythm of my orgasm, making me see stars. All while his cum spouts into me, filling me up and then some.

When we're both sated and his cock has deflated, he pulls out. I almost collapse right there, but he captures me in his arms and holds me steady, pressing sweet kisses on my back as he pants heavily.

"Don't worry," he whispers against my skin. "I've got you. Always."

My skin flushes with warmth and goose bumps because I know he means it.

With his arm wrapped around my body, holding me snuggly against him, I realize I don't want to be anywhere else but here right now. Right underneath his palm.

Claimed with his collar.

His.

TWENTY-EIGHT

CHASE

I pull open the drawer and take out the key, but as I fumble with it near her collar, she grabs my wrist.

"Can it stay on?" she asks, biting her lip.

I frown. "Why?"

She has always disliked how it felt. Has something changed?

"I like what it means."

Her words bring a warm smile to my face, and I grab her face and press a long-drawn-out kiss on her lips.

"I love you," I whisper.

She gives me a sugary sweet smile. "I ..."

I place a finger on her lips. "You don't have to say it. I

just want you to know how much you mean to me."

She nods. "I know."

I place another kiss on her forehead. "We can keep it on."

I tuck the key back into the drawer and grab her hand.

"I want you to decide," she says. "I'm yours."

I cock my head. "But I want you to be happy too."

She falls into my arms. "I am happy. Here. With you."

My body feels numb against her skin. Like her ray of sunshine scorches all the pain out of me and leaves nothing but compassion.

"Will you stay?" I ask.

She takes a deep breath. "Maybe."

"I promise I'll do everything in my power to make you happy." When she doesn't reply, I add, "I might even be able to stop myself from … killing. If it means you'll stay with me."

"You don't have to do that," she says. "I think I can live with it."

I swallow away the lump in my throat. "With a killer?"

"If it's only bad people … criminals."

"Yes. Only them. No innocent people." I breathe out a sigh of relief hearing her say that she's okay with me being … me.

"Am I free to leave whenever I want?" she asks.

I nod. "Always."

"Then I'll stay."

I close my eyes and smile as she buries her head in my

chest, and there we stay for a while. And it's okay. It's what we both need.

Slowly, I back away from the door and walk toward the bed. I hug her tight as we lie down. Her body snuggled against mine is the best feeling in the world. I can't stop sniffing to smell her scent, reveling in the idea that she's here. That she's mine. And that she's not going anywhere.

I don't mind if I have to beg for forgiveness the rest of my life. I know what I did can't be easily forgotten, but I will work hard every single day. She's worth it.

***

Syrena

Months later

As my heart begins to beat faster and faster, I clutch the paper tightly in my hand.

"Nervous?" Chase asks, driving along the road.

I nod. "Just a little." That's a lie. A lot. But I don't like showing just how much this means to me.

He places a hand on my leg. "You'll do great. It's going to be okay. I just know."

He always knows what I'm really feeling; I can't ever hide it from him. Just like he can't ever hide his true feelings from me.

I guess that's why we're so attached to each other. We both know what the other's weakness is … and it only makes us feel more powerful.

"We're here," he says as the car comes to a slow stop.

As I unbuckle, I take a deep breath and crumple up the paper in my hand, tucking it into my pocket. We no longer need the address if we've arrived.

"You wanna go in alone?" he asks.

"I don't know," I say, chewing my lip. I'm normally never this restless, but this situation isn't normal. Not even close.

"I think it's for the best." He leans over and kisses me on the cheek. "I'll wait out here until you come back."

"But what if I want to stay?"

There's a silence that seems to last an eternity.

"If that's what you want, I'll respect that," he says, and I can hear him smile.

I lean in to touch his face, feeling the ridges of his stubbly jawline, the smooth skin of his forehead, the thick lashes on his eyes, and the slick hair across his head. I memorize it … picture it in front of me, so I can always keep this in my thoughts. So I'll always have him with me, wherever I go. Knowing that makes me feel safe.

As my hands end on his lips, he presses a kiss to my palm and whispers, "Go … go meet your brother."

I nod and smile the brightest smile I have before opening the car door and jumping outside.

With renewed energy, I walk along the path, making sure I don't bump into things. A few more seconds pass before I ring the doorbell.

As someone's footsteps approach, my throat clamps up, and I cough out loud. Right then, someone opens the door, and I'm left scrambling for air.

I'm here.

I'm finally here.

I kept the paper with the address for so long, it almost faded, but I just couldn't push myself to actually go visit. Even when I had already deciphered the address using an app on my phone, I still couldn't bring myself to throw the paper away. It was the only tangible thing I had of them.

When I was still living at Roy's, the mere thought of facing them made me so anxious I could barely breathe. And when I went back to Chase, it never slipped my mind. I just couldn't bring myself to actually take that step.

It took me months to gather the courage and ask Chase to take me to their place.

And now the time is finally here.

"Sy…rena?"

Is that … Ella?

Suddenly, warm hands wrap around my neck, enveloping me with love and kindness, and I almost want to burst out into tears.

The last time we met, we were both still trapped behind glass, held prisoner by a cruel man whose only interest was to use us in whatever way he desired. And now we're finally free.

"Syrena!" she mutters, crying into my shoulder. "You're here. You're really here."

"Ella?" I mutter, overwhelmed by emotions. It feels so unreal.

She nods, whispering, "Yeah. It's me."

"Oh, my God …"

I blink as tears well up in my eyes.

I've never actually heard her talk.

When we were still in the cage, she never talked because she had selective mutism … Did she finally learn to speak to people?

"How did you find us? Are you okay? What happened to you?"

I have the exact same questions, and I don't even know whether to answer her first or to ask her first. So much is happening right now.

"I'm so sorry," she mutters, still whimpering.

I caress her back and say, "Don't be. It's not your fault."

"It was … because I couldn't … Graham took you … and then the buyer …"

She still feels guilty about the fact that Graham made her choose between giving her body to Cage when she didn't even know who he was yet and losing me. Graham used me as a bargaining chip against her. It was barbaric. But none of it was her fault, and I don't blame her for making the difficult decisions that she faced.

"Shhh …" I shush her. "It's okay. It happened. I don't

blame you for anything."

"But you were sold!" she says. "Did that man hurt you? Did you escape?"

I shake my head. "No. Well, yes, but no."

"What?"

"It's a long story." I chuckle.

"God, we have so much to catch up on," she says, pulling back.

"I'm sorry I didn't come sooner," I say. "I was afraid you'd—"

"Oh shush, you don't have to explain anything," she says. "How did you manage to come here? All by yourself?"

"No," I say, licking my lips. "Chase brought me."

"Chase … is that your …?" She leans in. "The one who bought you? Is he still here?"

"Yeah, but … he's not all bad," I say. "It's hard to explain. But he'll stay in the car, don't worry."

"Okay," she mumbles, caressing my arms. "God, it feels like ages since we last met."

"And finally in freedom," I add.

"That too."

"And you can talk," I mutter, still flabbergasted.

She laughs. "I guess we all changed."

That's true. So much has changed since we were in the cage. My whole world was turned upside down by Chase. But in a good way, I suppose. I feel much more free than I ever did before.

"Well, we'll have all the time in the world." She grabs

my hand. "C'mon. Cage is inside."

She drags me along with her, closing the door behind us before I can even say a word to Chase. But it's all right. I feel good about this, and I know he'll wait. Maybe even forever.

"Cage!" Ella calls out. "Syrena's here!"

"What?" a voice roars from upstairs.

A loud banging noise follows, and someone storms down so hard it feels as if there's an earthquake happening right now. Like a bunch of elephants are having a disco.

Except it's just him ... and his footsteps are coming right toward me.

I have no time to prepare for the massive arms pulling me into his embrace, practically choking me into a hug.

"Syrena, fuck ... you're here," he growls, hugging me so tight I feel as if I might pass out.

"Can't ... breathe," I mutter into his chest.

"Oh, right. Sorry." He puts me down on the floor, and I suck in some oxygen.

"Are you hurt?" he asks.

"No, I'm fine."

"Did *he* hurt you?" His voice darkens.

"No ... but it's a long story," I say.

"What does that mean?" he asks.

"That it was a bumpy ride getting here," Ella replies.

"A what?" he growls, making me laugh.

"I'll explain," I say, sighing. "I just don't even know where to start."

"Sit, sit," Ella says, "I'll make us some tea, so we can catch up."

She goes into the kitchen as Cage directs me to sit with him on the couch in their living room. When she comes back with tea and cookies, she tells me how she and Cage escaped and how they fell in love. I adore the story and can't wait to hear more, but she asks me about mine too. So I tell them everything that happened to me. From beginning to end, no details are left unmentioned. Except maybe the few times we had sex and just how dirty it was ... because fuck, whoever *can* talk about those things without blushing like crazy?

"So you're with him now?" she asks when I'm done talking. "Like ... a couple?"

I rub the back of my head. "Well, sort of."

"You want to stay with him?" she asks.

"I think so ... yes," I say, smiling. "I don't think I could live without him at this point, to be honest."

"Definite yes then," she muses.

Guess I've already made up my mind then. I'm going back with Chase. For a minute there, I was almost doubting whether I should, if I even could, but now that I've finally come here and talked to them, I'm only more convinced I belong with him.

I love these guys—they were everything I had for a moment in time—but we've all moved on. We all have our own lives now ... and that's okay.

We're free and happy. Just as we should be.

"She's blushing," Cage says.

"No, I'm not!" I hiss.

Ella giggles. "It's okay. I get it. Love works in mysterious ways."

I snort. "Can you be any more cheesy?"

"Way more," she retorts.

"Anyway, he's good to me. Or at least, he tries."

"Hey, I'm not complaining. It's great that you've found a place to call home." She places a hand on my lap. "As long as you're happy. That's all I want for you."

I smile. "Thank you. I ... I think I am, actually. I don't wanna be anywhere but around him."

I wasn't sure at first because I felt so guilty for having these feelings for Chase, but the more time I spend with him, the more that guilt begins to fade.

"Good," she replies. "And don't forget, you're always welcome here. And so is he." She clears her throat. "Maybe you can even bring him to meet us sometimes. Only when you're comfortable, of course. Someday, when you feel like it."

I agree. Today isn't the day, but maybe someday. "Sounds good," I say.

Suddenly, I hear the noise of a crying baby coming from above. Ella immediately jumps up and says, "Oh, be right back!"

She runs up the stairs and then comes back down again slowly. A baby makes some noise, but she shushes it softly, humming a song. "Syrena ..." she says as she stands in front of me. "Meet Forest."

I smile as she places the little boy in my hands. He's so big already, yet still so small compared to my hands. His head fits snuggly into my palm, and the soothing sounds of his mother's voice have lulled him straight back to sleep.

"He's sweet," I say.

"An angel," she says.

"My boy," Cage says proudly.

We all chuckle, and Ella takes him from my hands again after a while and places him back into the crib upstairs.

"There … he's asleep again.," she says.

"Did you have him after … being free?" I ask.

"Yeah. Although, I got pregnant in the compound," she says, and I can hear the pain in her voice. "But it's okay. I love him and Cage to bits."

She sits down on the couch again, and I think they're hugging.

I just can't help but think about how much of a family they are … and how I'm still keeping this giant secret from them. They should know. I just never know when the right time is to tell them, and it's making my heart palpitate.

"What's wrong?" Ella suddenly asks.

"Nothing, I just … have something to tell you," I say.

"What?" she asks.

"Chase told me … Graham admitted that I was … his daughter." The words come out in one difficult breath.

"What?" Cage gets up from the couch.

"My mother was held captive by Graham. Our mother."

I grab my hair and pull it away to show them my neck. "We know because of this birthmark."

"Oh my," Ella mutters. "Cage …"

"I've got that too," he says, his voice low. "On my inner thigh."

"I swallow away the lump in my throat. "Graham lied to us all."

"You're my sister?" His voice cracks.

I nod, tears welling up in my eyes.

Suddenly, he goes to his knees in front of me and wraps his arms around my neck again, only this time without squeezing. It's loving, warm, and as he holds me tight, the tears begin to fall.

"I have a sister too," he mutters. "I didn't even know."

"It's okay. None of us did," I reply. "Graham didn't want us to know. It's how he held power over us."

"But he hurt you. He tried to use you for …" Ella says, unable to finish her sentence.

"I know."

"And he still sold you!" Ella shouts.

"I know, it's crazy," I say. "I'm sorry, I should've contacted you to tell you sooner. Should've come to you with this."

"No, don't apologize," Cage growls into my ear. "You *don't* apologize."

He hugs me even tighter, and we stay there for a while until my tears have dried and his heart is no longer beating out of his chest.

"Our mother, she ..." I mutter.

"Shh ... it's okay," Cage says. "You can tell us when you're ready."

I appreciate the gesture and take a deep breath, trying not to hiccup from my own pent-up tears.

After a while, Cage asks, "So do you know about my, I mean *our* brother too?"

I nod, wiping my face. "Yes, what's his name? Is he here too?"

"His name's Lock," Ella says. "But he lives on an island by himself."

"That's what Chase said too," I say.

"I'll contact him. Tell him about you," Cage says.

"You sure?" I ask.

"He has to know he has a sister," he adds.

I nod, licking my lips. "Not one ... but two brothers. And here I was thinking I had no family."

Chuckling, Ella joins in the hug, and says, "You always had a family, Syrena. We were right here, waiting for you to come home. And now you finally did."

EPILOGUE

CHASE

Syrena stayed inside for ages. I don't know what they talked about, but I assumed she told them about her ordeal. From the cage all the way to me ... and maybe even about being brother and sister. About their mother and the bond they share.

Of course, she'd need the time, and I fully respect that.

But I never expected her to come back to my car after everything was said and done.

It was humbling, to say the least. I didn't even know how to respond, so instead, I drove off.

I already know what choice she made, and that's all I'll ever need.

She's free to do what she wants. Anytime she wants to come back here, I'll drive her myself. I won't get in her way. And she knows that.

It's silent as we drive back home.

I don't have anything to say to her, and neither does she.

We don't have to speak the words because we already know them by heart.

I'm smitten, and she's lost to me ...

We're part of the same game, the same endless loop. She needs me, and I need her. And even though we once hated that very part of ourselves, we've come to live with it.

In fact, when I look at her, all I can do is smile.

I can honestly say I'm happier than I've ever been. Not because my life has gone so smoothly, but because even through all the bad shit, I still have her. Because no matter how wrong things get, she's still here with me ...

Out of her own free will.

I didn't force her. Didn't ask her. Didn't make her follow me or come back home with me.

She came to me because she wanted to. Because it was her decision. Her choice ... to fall for me.

This was never about me changing my ways or figuring out the truth about my own selfish needs. I always knew who I was, and I knew that nothing would ever change.

I was just hoping that I could ... because who would ever love a monster like me?

But she does.

She loves me ...

No ifs. No buts.

No shame. No hiding who I am.

She knows what she came back to and accepts it without question. She accepts *me*.

And ultimately … that's all I'll ever need.

***

Syrena

The car comes to a stop on the dirt road.

"Are you sure you want to do this?" he asks.

I take a deep breath and roll down the windows, smelling that familiar scent of the red sand. The scorching sun heats my skin, but it feels warm. Inviting.

I turn toward Chase and say, "Absolutely."

"I don't want you to regret this," he says.

I place a hand on his cheek and caress him. "I trust you."

He places a hand on top of mine and sighs. Then he nods and takes the key from his pocket, unlocking the metal collar around my neck. When it drops to my legs, and as the fresh air brushes along my skin, I gasp.

And then I open the door and bolt out.

Into the nothing … in the middle of nowhere, where no

one will ever find us.

Like a deer on the run, I go as fast as my legs will take me.

The hard breaths coming from my throat drive me into a frenzy. When I hear his rapid footsteps behind me, panic starts to shoot through my veins, making me run even faster.

Adrenaline pumps through my body as I skid through the dry sand, which whips up into my throat.

I cough as tears well up in my eyes, but I continue to run. I have no choice.

This is it. This is the moment I've been waiting for.

The run of my life.

The final showdown.

And in the exact same place as before ... the canyon.

This place is still unfamiliar to me, but my feet are much steadier than before, and simple rocks won't bring me down. I'm not drugged, not weighed down by clothes, and not under the influence or whatever else that could hamper me.

This is how it should've been. How he desired it to go.

The ultimate game of the hunter and the prey.

And he's right there, following behind me, ready to strike.

Fear creeps up into my bones, but I refuse to let it get to me. I refuse to give in to the emotions. They'll only hold me back.

But the longer I run, the more my legs begin to wear out, the pain beginning to show in my movements. One misstep is all it takes and I'm on the ground.

"Got you …" he growls, grasping my legs.

I groan as I lift my head, but he's quickly on top of me, preventing me from getting up from the ground.

Suddenly, a knife is pressed right near my throat.

"Nowhere to run, nowhere to hide," he murmurs, his tongue dipping out to lick my neck.

I shiver. My heart palpitates as I hold my breath.

A sharp sting lingers on my skin, then a warm flow. Blood.

His lips cover the spot, sucking up the liquid.

He moans.

The blade drops to the ground.

I breathe out a sigh of relief, a smile forming on my lips.

"Thank you," I whisper.

He pauses for a second, then whispers into my ear. "No … thank you for this pleasure."

I bite my lip as he continues teasing me, his lips warming my skin as he showers me with luscious kisses.

I lift my head as he laps up the last drops of blood. His hand curls underneath my chin, pulling me up until his lips crash on mine and we're lost in an eternal battle of lust once again.

As our mouths unlock for a quick breath, I mutter, "I love you."

I don't even have to think about it.

Don't have to feel shame for the words that roll off my tongue.

Because they're the truth ... and that's the only thing that matters.

Us.

A warm, soft smile meets my lips as his tongue briefly dips out as if to savor the words. "I love you too."

And then he goes right back to completely ravaging me.

This is how it always goes. How it's supposed to go. How I prefer it.

Him, loving me, taking me whenever he likes and however he sees fit.

Soon, his hands find their way to my thighs, parting them, invading my privacy. And I don't mind it one bit. I love what he does, how possessive he is, how controlling he is. How hard it makes him when I try to resist.

The chase is what turns him on. What drives his very existence.

But this time, it was my choice, not his.

I asked him to do this. To replace the bad memories with good ones.

To give me his all.

And he does.

Every ... single ... inch.

EXCERPT OF HOTEL O

Kat

With a cup of steaming coffee, I close the curtains and sit down behind my laptop. Without thinking twice, I turn on the browser and go to the chat site I always go to when I get bored. It's late at night, and I've finished all my work for tomorrow, so why not enjoy myself? I've earned this.

I enter a name and a birth date and log in.

Name: NaughtyKitten.

Age: Twenty-seven.

Currently Wearing: Blue tank top.

My profile is blank with the exception of two small tidbits.

As dirty as can be. Humiliate me.

It might sound wrong, but hey … that's what these chat sites are for. People don't discuss the weather or work here. No one cares who you are in real life, and we don't want to know you. We just want to have fun.

That's why this site exists … and why I love it so much.

Being cooped up in my little apartment with little breathing room in my private life has made me eager to try new things, and this … this little gem right here is proving to be one of my favorite things to do late at night.

Or any time a day, really.

I'm a sucker for exciting things. Or rather … dicks.

I can't help myself. Growing up so sheltered has me wanting to try out literally everything since I've been living on my own. Nothing's too thrilling for me. Mostly in the sex department.

That's what you get when you're not allowed to date, and your parents are protective as hell. You resort to being a sneaky bitch and having boyfriends climb up to your room in the middle of the night. But all that fades compared to what I want. To what I'm thinking of when I fondle myself.

I want to be taken. Used. In every way possible.

I've wanted it for so long, but any man who came into my life after I moved out was never up to the task. Most men shy away when I tell them my dirtiest wishes. Guess I'm a lot of maintenance.

Which is why I resort to online stuff instead.

This makes it easier to quit, without even having to say a

word.

You can just exit the window and be done with it. Quiet and easily. No one will ever know it was me, which is the most important factor. If people only knew what I really like, they'd run for the hills. Hell, if my boss found out, he'd probably fire me on the spot for lewd behavior.

Especially if he knew I sometimes go to this chatroom at work.

But no one has to find out.

It's my dirty little secret.

And now it will be *his* too.

Because someone has already pinged me for a private conversation ... and when I check out his profile, I'm pleasantly surprised.

Name: D.

Age: Thirty-three.

Currently Wearing: Suit. Commando underneath.

Description: No commitment. No strings. Just pleasure ... and you doing everything I tell you to.

A wicked grin spreads on my lips as I take a sip of my coffee and press the accept button.

His picture appears too now. Second surprise of the day. It's not a dick pic. It's a picture of him buttoning up his well-ironed shirt.

Well, now I've seen it all.

A man who won't show off his dick the very first chance he gets? Color me intrigued.

And not just that, but he looks rather ... buff too.

Because I can definitely see those pecs underneath his shirt.

My mouth is already watering.

But I have to remind myself that this is only a fantasy. Once I close the laptop, he'll be gone forever.

With a smirk on my face, I start typing. If he won't be the first to actually say something, I'll break the ice. I'm not that shy ... but maybe he is.

NaughtyKitten: Hey.

No response.

I can see him typing, though. What kind of greeting takes so long to write?

D: Take off your clothes.

I frown.

What's this then? Going all out right away?

NaughtyKitten: No 'hi' first? Maybe we should talk first? See if we match up?

D: I take no pleasure in formalities. Are you here to play or not?

I take another sip of my coffee and narrow my eyes. He's very straightforward. I haven't decided yet whether I like it or not, but I'll play along. See where it goes.

NaughtyKitten: Yes. What are you here for?

D: To get off.

NaugtyKitten: Then we have a mutual interest.

D: My interest is you. Now take off your clothes.

NaugtyKitten: What gave you the impression I'll do what you say?

I lick my lips and put my coffee down as I wait for his

answer.

D: Because you want to. Because you asked for it.
NaughtyKitten: Where?

It takes him a while to respond.

It's not a text.

It's a picture … of my own profile description.

D: Was this a lie?

NaughtyKitten: It wasn't. But I like to know who I'm speaking to as well. What do you like?

D: You. Naked. Fingering yourself for me on camera.

I'm not gonna lie, that actually made my pussy clench.

NaughtyKitten: Okay. But what makes you think I will trust you with pictures?

D: You don't have to trust me. I'm just here to humiliate you. Now do as I say.

I swallow away the lump in my throat as my finger hovers over the mouse button. I'm tempted to close the chat right there and then, but something stops me. The curious side in me refuses to let go. I've never talked to a man like him, so straightforward with what he wants. It's almost … scary.

Scary exciting.

Too exciting.

But then I remember I've been living the norm because other people want me to. Not because I want to. I want to be filthy. I want to be someone's plaything. I want this. Now.

So I smile and start to type again.

NaughtyKitten: Tell me what to do.

D: Send me a picture of your tits.

I rub my lips and contemplate it for a few seconds. Should I? It's not like I haven't sent them to a dude before. I always make sure to blur out or cut off my face, of course. I don't want anyone to recognize me. There's really no reason not to. Except … I normally talk with a guy before immediately jumping into the sex chats with them.

But I guess this guy likes things to move along.

Okay. No problem. Challenging myself to push my boundaries is fun.

I check my laptop for any pics I already took and find one of my boobs, which I send to him.

It doesn't take him long to respond.

D: That's not from today.

I frown. How can he tell?

D: Wrong shirt.

Oh … Right. I forgot you had to enter what you're wearing.

D: Are you trying to fool me?

NaughtyKitten: No.

D: How will I know if you really look like the picture on your profile?

NaughtyKitten: It's me. Promise.

D: You're really a naughty kitten … playing dirty.

It's a picture of my boobs covered by a small pink bra, which is enough to lure the men without giving away my best asset. Obviously, he paid attention. Smart.

D: I won't accept a pre-made picture. I need the real deal. Now. Write the letter D on your left tit. Make your nipples nice and hard. Twist your right nipple. Send me a picture. Nude.

Holy shit. He really is demanding. I like it.

I lift my tank top to expose my boobs and grab a marker, penning the letter down on my left one. Then I make my nipples hard and twist the right one, taking a picture with my phone. I immediately upload it to my laptop where I edit it until my face is no longer visible.

One ... two ... three seconds of doubt. It's sent.

My whole body is trembling with delicious vibes as I wait for his response. I don't know why I always like this moment so much. What excites me about a man seeing me for the first time. Maybe it's the forbidden aspect ... that makes me feel really, really dirty.

D: Good ... Now this is what I wanted to see.
NaughtyKitten: Do you like my tits?
D: Oh, yes. I'm already hard as a rock.

My pussy thumps again at the thought. I wonder what he looks like.

NaughtyKitten: Send me a pic.
D: You listen to me. Not the other way around. Remember what you came here for.

I frown. Well, isn't he cheerful. Though, I suppose he's right ... in a way.

D: But I'll humor you this time. Because I like you.

Not too long after, he sends me a picture ... but not of his dick. No, it's his button-up shirt, the same one from his profile picture, pulled up all the way to the top of his neck. All I see are ... abs ... but my God, do they look lickable. A small trail of hair leads downward from his navel, past his V-line, right to where I want to put my mouth.

D: Like what you see?

NaughtyKitten: Oh, yes. Although I was hoping for more.

D: Patience is a virtue.

NaughtyKitten: I'm too dirty to be patient. Or good, for that matter. It's in my name.

D: Sinful ... I like that.

I take another sip of my coffee, which isn't even hot anymore. Shit. I completely forgot about it in the heat of the moment. Guess I'm a sucker for a filthy fuck ... and this guy certainly strikes me as one.

D: How naughty are you?

Is this a trick question?

NaughtyKitten: As naughty as you want me to be.

D: Do you have a video camera?

NaughtyKitten: I have my phone. Is that good?

D: Film yourself while you play with your pussy. I want to see it all. Up. Close.

I almost jump up from my seat and grab my phone, then take off my panties. They're already soaked. Jesus, am I this easy? Yes, I am, and I don't even care.

I sit down and place the camera near my legs, so it only

films my pussy and not any higher. But before I start, I send him another message.

NaughtyKitten: Ready.

D: Open your legs as wide as you can. Touch your clit. Make yourself wet.

Fuck, I already am. But I still begin rubbing myself anyway. I can't help it, the thought of someone watching soon makes me so goddamn horny. I can't wait for him to see it … I wonder if it'll make him come.

The camera is recording as I flick my clit and moan out loud. I hope it picks up my sounds. I'm already soaked and swollen when he keeps typing more.

D: Finger yourself. First with one. Then with two. And when you do, think about how dirty you're being. How bad you are.

Fuck, yes. I love it when they talk dirty.

It only makes me moan harder.

I shove a finger in and imagine it's him doing it while he claims my mouth. I imagine him making me come and then shoving his dick into my mouth, forcing me to swallow him down. God, I want it all. Every inch of filth.

D: Finger yourself until you come all over the chair and show me the wetness on your fingers. I want to see how much of a filthy slut you really are.

Fuck me, when they start calling me names, I'm begging for mercy.

I don't know what it is about being humiliated that turns me on so much, but it does.

D: Come like the slut you are. Come all over your hands and the camera.

One second is all it takes for the explosions to fill my body and take over. And I sink into the chair as my body convulses, my legs quaking with need. Fuck ... what I wouldn't do for a dick right about now.

NaughtyKitten: Fuck ... Yes.
D: Did you come? Show me.

I hold my fingers in front of the camera and then turn it off with my other hand. Then I wash my hands and get back to my seat. I contemplate shutting off the chat. I got my fill. Then again ... I haven't met a lot of dudes like him online. I don't want this to stop.

So I upload the video from my phone to my laptop and play it to make sure it doesn't show my face before I send it to him. When I click the button to send, my heart begins to race. What if he finds out who I am? What if he uses it against me? Makes me lose my job? Or worse ...

A shiver runs down my spine.

It's already too late. I already pressed the button. He's already downloading it as we speak.

I just have to believe in him and stop worrying about the consequences. I wanted this. I needed the excitement. So I'd better accept whatever happens. It's part of the thrill.

When he starts typing again, I blow out a sigh of relief.

D: Tell me what you thought of when you fucked yourself like that.

NaughtyKitten: You.

D: What did you imagine me doing to you?

NaughtyKitten: I thought of your fingers, pushing inside me. You, making me come. And you ... shoving your dick down my throat until I can't breathe.

D: You like that, filthy slut?

NaughtyKitten: I love being used.

D: You're still wet, aren't you?

NaughtyKitten: Yes. And I'm purring for more.

D: You're more perfect than I thought.

Perfect? What does he mean? Does he intend to make this into more than a one-time thing?

D: I'm rubbing my cock right now ... watching you play with yourself. Does that turn you on?

NaughtyKitten: Fuck, yes. I want to see.

D: If you're naughty, I might show it to you.

NaughtyKitten: I'll do anything. Just give it to me.

D: Anything?

NaughtyKitten: Yes.

D: Then let's make this a rain check.

I suck in a breath and pause. Where is he going with this?

NaughtyKitten: ??

D: Next time you log on, you contact me. We'll see how much you want to see this.

NaughtyKitten: Next time?

D: Do you work?

NaughtyKitten: Yes. But we're not supposed to talk about that.

This is so strange ... a guy who wants to do this again. Also, it's not technically allowed, because it could put members in jeopardy. Yet I can't stop talking to him. I want more. I want so much more.

D: So you have a lunch break then?

NaughtyKitten: Yes. Twelve thirty.

D: Good.

D: Monday. Twelve thirty. Same names. Same outfit. And bring a dildo or a vibrator.

NaughtyKitten: But I'm wearing inappropriate stuff. And a dildo? At work?

D: You will wear this and bring the dildo because I want you to.

NaughtyKitten: But ...

D: Humiliation, remember? It's in your profile.

Well, he isn't wrong. I just ... don't know if I can do it.

D: Do what I want, and I'll give it to you. Every ... inch.

Just the thought makes me drool.

But before I can even say okay or no, he's already canceled the chat and gone offline.

Hotel O: Coming Soon!

THANK YOU FOR READING!

Thank you so much for reading Chased. I hope you enjoyed the story!

For updates about upcoming books, please visit my website, www.clarissawild.blogspot.com or sign up for my newsletter here: www.bit.ly/clarissanewsletter.

I'd love to talk to you! You can find me on Facebook: www.facebook.com/ClarissaWildAuthor, make sure to click LIKE. You can also join the Fan Club: www.facebook.com/groups/FanClubClarissaWild/ and talk with other readers!

Enjoyed this book? You could really help out by leaving a review on Amazon and Goodreads. Thank you!

ALSO BY CLARISSA WILD

Dark Romance
Delirious Series
Killer & Stalker
Mr. X
Twenty-One
Ultimate Sin
VIKTOR
Indecent Games Series
FATHER
CAGED & LOCKED

New Adult Romance
Fierce Series
Blissful Series
Ruin

Erotic Romance
The Billionaire's Bet Series
Enflamed Series
Unprofessional Bad Boys Series

Visit Clarissa Wild's website for current titles.
http://clarissawild.blogspot.com

ABOUT THE AUTHOR

Clarissa Wild is a New York Times & USA Today Bestselling author, best known for the dark Romance novel Mr. X. Her novels include the Fierce Series, the Delirious Series, Stalker Duology, Twenty-One (21), Ultimate Sin, Viktor, the Unprofessional Bad Boys Series, RUIN, the Indecent Games Series, Father, CAGED, and LOCKED. She is an avid reader and writer of sexy stories about hot men and feisty women. Her other loves include her furry cat friend and learning about different cultures. In her free time she enjoys watching all sorts of movies, reading tons of books and cooking her favorite meals.

Want to be informed of new releases and special offers? Sign up for Clarissa Wild's newsletter on her website clarissawild.blogspot.com.

Visit Clarissa Wild on Amazon for current titles.

Printed in Great Britain
by Amazon